TEMPTING THE BLUESTOCKING

A Gentleman Courtesans Novella

VICTORIA VALE

PROLOGUE

The clamor and cloying stench of the London docks faded into obscurity as Edward Norton crossed the threshold of Norton & Rivers Line. The dimly lit interior and cold hearth struck him as being particularly depressing, seizing him with the urge to duck back out into the chilly morning. He could hail a hackney and be on his way to his lodgings in a matter of minutes. But, the sign above the door proclaimed for all the world that this place was now his responsibility. Besides, he had avoided his duty long enough. The remains of what had once been his father's business weren't going to fix themselves, nor would the piles of his debts be paid if he went on pretending they didn't exist. He had danced on the edge of avoidance long enough, and as the eldest of his siblings it fell to him to set matters right. Of course, he had no notion of how he might do that, but if he didn't mend this no one else would.

His brother, Jacob, was just barely out of university and hardly knew his right foot from his left, let alone anything that might prove useful in bringing a failing shipping company back from the brink of devastation. As for Edward's sister; she was the typical unwed gentry chit, her head filled with whatever nonsense a girl is taught when it comes to the pursuit of a husband. Their fates rested upon his shoulders as heavily as his own.

Doffing his hat, he searched the establishment. Two imposing desks faced each other from opposite sides of the large front room, one of them strewn with documents and ledgers in a jumble that made his left eye twitch. The other was startlingly bare by contrast, a fine layer of dust coating its surface, while cobwebs stretched between the slats of the wooden chair behind it. The abandoned desk confronted Edward with a reminder that this wouldn't rest solely on him had his father not chased away a perfectly good business partner. As it stood, the 'Rivers' half of Norton & Rivers had retired to Paris on the amount his part of the line had been bought for. Which left Edward between the hammer and the anvil at present—with the mistakes of his father beneath him, and his own lack of funds battering him with overwhelming force.

Seated behind the mess-strewn desk was Mr. Jasper Bullock, his father's former solicitor. Short and reed slender, he reminded Edward of a bird with his sharply pointed nose and close-set eyes. He stood as Edward approached, beady eyes going wide as if with alarm.

Edward knew the unrelenting black he wore did nothing for his coloring, and that lack of sleep had him looking a fright ... but, honestly, the man had nothing to fear. It wasn't as if he'd walked into this office without knowing to expect the worst.

Forcing a grim smile, he offered Bullock a hand. "Good morning. Thank you for taking the time to meet me. I realize you aren't obligated to help me, but as the man who knows more than anyone else what the state of affairs is here ..."

Bullock nodded several times in swift succession, his movements disjointed and jerky. "Yes, yes ... it is no trouble. And, as you said, I can give you the clearest picture of what you have inherited."

Edward wanted to point out that what he'd inherited was akin to having a boulder tied to his ankles before being dropped into the ocean. But, Bullock did not look like the sort of man who would appreciate his brand of wry, self-deprecating humor, so he refrained.

He procured the chair from behind the empty desk, swiping away the cobwebs before carrying it to where Bullock waited.

"Shall we begin?"

Bullock cleared his throat and resumed his seat, shuffling several documents before glancing at Edward from the corner of his eye.

"Mr. Norton, I must warn you ... well, I knew things were bad, but I could never have realized just how—"

"Bullock," Edward cut in. "I loved my father dearly, bless his soul, but the man was a horrible businessman. On my desk at home are dozens of bills from my father's creditors. The sums are so astronomical it is a wonder he wasn't carted off to debtor's prison. There is nothing you could tell me about the state of Norton and Rivers that would shock me. So, please get on with it. Tell me everything and speak plainly, so I can get to work fixing this mess."

Bullock had been staring at him in a stunned sort of stupor, but quickly snapped out of it, clearing his throat yet again. "Very well, I shall speak plainly. In truth, Mr. Norton, without a large influx of capital there is no feasible way to keep the line afloat. As it stands, your father made the worst possible decision by buying out Mr. Rivers' share. It marked the end of the business' most profitable years."

Edward pinched the bridge of his nose and sighed. "I warned him not to do it, and even tried to talk Rivers out of selling his share. But, I can hardly blame the man. He and Father were old school friends, but where Rivers had a head for business, my father most certainly did not. The man wanted to cut his losses and get out before he went down right along with Father. It's no more than I would have done."

Mr. Bullock grimaced. "Without Rivers here, your father ran the line on his own, and his mismanagement is responsible for its decline. As of now, you've only one ship that's fit enough to make the voyage along its route, and even it is in dire need of repairs. Its crew is sparse as well, many of the seaman having abandoned ship when cargo and profits became scarce."

Edward drew in a deep breath, a slow pounding beginning in one of his temples. "Norton and Rivers used to have a fleet of ships, a dozen at least. What happened to them?"

Bullock lifted a register from which he read aloud. "One overtaken and commandeered by pirates somewhere along the East Indies route, another sunk with its cargo in a storm off the coast of the Mediterranean. All the others simply cannot be taken to sea without repairs and men willing to crew them."

Edward didn't want to ask his next question aloud; he really didn't. But these were things he needed to know if he had any hope of cleaning up his father's mess.

"If the records are to be believed, some of these ships haven't seen a voyage in as long as a year. Why have they gone so long without repairs?"

One would think repairing ships would be a priority around here— more vessels coming and going from London with cargo meant more profits, which could eventually mean more ships, better ships, faster ships. But, his father's mind had never been so linear. The man had thought in circles and ellipses and tangles so convoluted no sane person could follow.

Bullock offered him a stack of familiar-looking documents that had Edward's heart plummeting. They were receipts for the cost of timber and other supplies, as well as for the services of those who repaired and equipped ships for their voyages. Some of them dated back a year or more, which would explain why so many of their vessels had been out of commission for so long.

"So, we owe these suppliers and craftsmen so much money they've stopped doing business with us until such time as they are paid?"

"Precisely," Bullock replied. "As well, there is the matter of the rents on your warehouses. They went unpaid for so long that Norton and Rivers no longer has the capacity to store cargo. So even if your ships could voyage to other ports and return with goods ..."

"We'd have no bloody place to put them," Edward grumbled, suddenly in need of a stiff drink.

"Correct."

"Would I also be correct to assume that all of this has resulted in the loss of the company's reputation? I would imagine most of our loyal clients have now turned to a line better fit to meet their needs."

"Unfortunately, you have the right of it. Business has come to a standstill without warehouses, ships, or crews. And without the funds to fix the ships, rent the warehouses, and hire crews ..."

"We're rolled up." Edward issued a short, sarcastic bark of laughter. "*I'm* rolled up ... ruined. Damn it all to hell."

Bullock didn't reply, simply giving him a look that portrayed the deepest of sympathies. No wonder the man had been reluctant to tell him the truth about how dire his straits were.

He now felt as if he'd been thrown into the depths of the ocean with no notion of how to swim, and even if he could the boulder tied his angles dragged him down into the depths. He was university educated, but had never actually worked for a living, since Norton & Rivers had pulled in enough capital to support the entire family. Or, at least, it had *seemed* to support them. Only after he'd grown old enough to truly pay attention did he realize that his family merely displayed an illusion of wealth outwardly, while in truth they'd been drowning in debt, suffocating under the weight of his father's mismanagement for decades. He'd tried to offer his father assistance, and had even begged the man to make him his partner once Rivers had left, but Edwards's pleas had fallen on deaf ears. Aside from being a terrible businessman, his father had suffered from tender pride and stubbornness that would put a mule to shame. He'd insisted he had things well in hand, and had refused Edward's help.

For a scant few seconds, Edward wrestled with an intense loathing for his father. His jaw clenched until it ached, and his body practically hummed with the force of his anger at the man who had died a few short weeks ago, leaving Edward to clean up the mess he'd made of all their lives.

But then, he remembered all the good things about his father that had always seemed to overshadow his flaws. His tolerance for Caroline's choosiness when it came to the selection of a husband. His patience with Jacob, whose lack of direction had worried their mother to no end. He'd been the best father three children could ask for in all the ways that counted, and Edward supposed he could be forgiven for failing at managing his money and his business.

As Edward stood to shake the solicitor's hand, his mind already raced through a number of solutions to a problem he feared he might never solve. However, each idea was tossed aside as he realized they all required the one thing he did not have at the moment: a large influx of funds.

SEVERAL HOURS LATER, EDWARD SAT ACROSS FROM AN OLD FRIEND IN a coffee house in Covent Garden. He could hardly afford the expense of indulging in the curry and rice steaming before him, but neither could he afford to continue paying the woman who cooked his meals at home. So, it hardly mattered, did it?

He'd developed a fondness for Indian cuisine while visiting the home of a friend from university. The man's father had been an officer of the East India Company, who'd returned to England with a cook from Calcutta. During his time with his friend's family, Edward had experienced various curries and channa masala, finding he enjoyed the robust flavors.

It was to curry he turned now, finding comfort in the dish as he stared morosely at the man sitting across from him. The Honourable Mr. Hugh Radcliffe had befriended him at university, and the two often found themselves in one another's company. As a gentleman lacking a title or any familial connection to the *beau monde*, Edward had very few friends of the peerage. But, Hugh often reminded Edward that he could hardly be considered *ton* any longer—not after being disowned for pursuing a career as a portraitist. He'd been cast out of his family, his financial situation as dire as Edward's—perhaps even more so.

"I don't know what the bloody hell I'm supposed to do," he muttered between bites of curry with a shake of his head. "The old man left nothing, not even a business that could be salvaged to create some sort of living for our family. It seems wiser to burn it all down to ashes as opposed to trying to raise it from the dead."

Hugh gave him a sympathetic look while reaching for a flat disk of naan bread. "Could you just sell it to someone looking for a project—

some enterprising gentleman with deep pockets who could transform the business into a steady stream of income?"

Edward scoffed. "He'd be purchasing a mountain of debt on top of a defunct fleet of ships. Said gentleman would also have to be completely mutton-headed."

"You make a good point. Perhaps a money lender of some kind?"

"One who will charge me interest I can't afford, and extract my teeth one by one when I'm unable to pay him back? No, thank you."

Hugh chewed, seeming to mull over his words before he spoke. He looked as if he were on the verge of disclosing some scandalous revelation, and despite his morose situation, Edward found his curiosity piqued.

"I think ... I might know of a way you could earn a large sum of money in a matter of months. But, I cannot tell you what it is. Not yet."

Edward scowled, taking a closer look at his friend. He hadn't seen Hugh in months, and ought to have noticed the changes. His friend's outmoded, ill-fitting clothing had been replaced with perfectly tailored togs, most of which looked brand spanking new. He flaunted a fresh haircut, and had even gained back the weight he'd lost when lean months had seen him taking meager meals. Hugh was a new man, and it would seem this mysterious source of money had been responsible for the change.

A dart of hope arrowed through him and Edward leaned forward. "Why can't you tell me what it is?"

Hugh glanced about as if he didn't want to be overheard. "The person who runs this...agency...he has the final say when it comes to who can be invited to join us. But, the money is good. Better than the allowance I was once entitled to from my father. It might not solve all your problems but it could be enough to pay some of the creditors, perhaps get your ships up and running again."

Edward's spine snapped straight, excitement flooding him in a rush. Working ships would attract crews to sail them, which might, in turn, earn back their clients along with a few new ones. Maybe there would be enough to rent a warehouse. If he could start generating some sort of income, things wouldn't have to be so grave. His family name needn't continue to be synonymous with bad business, not if he could prove that Norton & Rivers was making strides under new management. Caroline and Jacob could have a secure future.

"Whatever it is, I'll do it," he said. "Tell your associate I'll meet any requirements he might have."

Hugh held a hand up to silence him and leaned closer, lowering his voice. "The agency is kept secret for a reason. The work we do is the sort that could cause a scandal unlike anything London has ever seen if we're exposed. You have to understand ... those of us who founded it were desperate. We needed the money and, like you, had no other recourse. It's been a year since we began, and now I'm flush enough to support myself until I can have my work displayed in the Royal Academy's Summer Exhibition."

Now Edward really must know just what Hugh had done to earn himself that sort of blunt. The man had stood weeks away from being evicted from his suite of bachelor's rooms the last time they'd spoken. Now, he was about Town dressed in the height of fashion and looking as well-fed as ever.

"I'm not concerned with the scandalous nature of this business," he vowed. "I want in, Hugh. Whatever it takes."

Hugh nodded. "Fine, meet me at Number 8 Clarges Street at noon tomorrow. My associate will be there, and we'll discuss the particulars."

Edward found himself once again taken aback. The address Hugh had given him was one far too fashionable for a man in Hugh's position. That must mean he truly had done well for himself this past year. Whatever he'd been up to, Edward would follow in his footsteps. So long as it wasn't moonlighting as a highwayman, he saw no reason to balk at whatever unseemly tasks it might entail.

The mystery of it confounded him for the rest of the night, long after he parted ways with Hugh. It robbed Edward of sleep, his mind racing as he pondered all the various schemes he might find himself pulled into. It became a distraction he could not distance his mind from, as was evidenced by his woolgathering over breakfast.

His sister had frowned at him, annoyed that he'd barely heard a word of her complaining over the sparse fare available to them. While Caroline was well aware of the family's current state of near poverty, years of comfortable if not extravagant living had made her rather spoiled. She wanted something other than chicken for dinner, as it was all there had been for nigh on a week. Instead of scolding her for her ungratefulness, Edward had simply smiled and told her that she might just have her wish soon enough. If Hugh's improved circumstances were any indication, he'd be able to replace her worn, patched gowns, which she never ceased reminding him were at least two Seasons out of fashion. She'd expressed curiosity about his new enterprise, but ceased asking questions once he made it clear he wouldn't discuss it. Caroline seemed pacified with the knowledge that Edward did not intend to simply sit back while their circumstances grew worse.

He'd left her to attend his meeting, a spring in his step as he took the long walk to Clarges Street. He could have paid for a hackney coach, but preferred to save his limited funds after his splurge on dinner last evening.

A footman greeted him at the front door of Hugh's townhome, which sat amid a row of elegant residences. So, not only could his old friend now afford new lodgings in a fashionable part of town, he also had servants in his employ. Edward's curiosity had reached its peak by the time he was ushered into a drawing room, where Hugh awaited him along with another man Edward had never met before.

"Ed, this is Mr. Benedict Sterling ... Ben, this is my good friend, Mr. Edward Norton."

Mr. Sterling rose from where he'd sat sprawled in an armchair, standing at an impressive height. Despite his scruffy jaw, bristling sideburns, and mop of unruly light blond hair, his mode of dress suggested wealth and class.

"A pleasure to meet you," Edward said, extending a hand to Mr. Sterling.

Rather than take him up on the offered handshake, the man paced around Edward in a slow circle, looking him over as if inspecting a sculpture or some other such inanimate object.

"He isn't particularly tall, but he isn't necessarily short, either," he mumbled, a hand braced at his chin.

Edward cast Hugh a quizzical glance, but his friend merely nodded as if in encouragement, remaining silent. Benedict paused behind him and murmured something about 'nice calves', causing Edward's ears to grow hot. Not the first time he'd received such a compliment, but never from another man, and never under such odd circumstances.

Benedict came around to face him, arms braced over his chest. "He's handsome, like you said."

That statement was directed at Hugh, who nodded his agreement.

"He's a gentleman," Hugh said. "Not a peer, but still well bred."

"Can you dance?" Benedict asked, finally addressing Edward directly.

"Well enough," he hedged, realizing he'd come to this meeting grossly unprepared. What the devil was happening here?

"Would you say that women find you charming?"

Edward furrowed his brow. "Well, I've never thought to ask. As I do not come with a fortune or prestigious family name, I can't pretend to be the most sought after of bachelors, but am never short on female companionship in social situations."

Benedict cast a glance at Hugh. "And you're certain we can trust him? He'll be discreet?"

"I can vouch for him," Hugh replied. "He needs the funds, Ben."

"Very well. He's hired."

Edward fought the swirling mixture of elation and confusion tearing through him. While he was glad to have been accepted so readily, he still had no idea what he'd be doing to earn a living.

"What exactly is it I'm hired to do?" he asked, finally finding his voice.

Hugh gestured for him to sit, taking his own chair nearby. Benedict, who remained standing, continued to hold the reins as the person in charge of this little meeting.

"You'll be matched with a young lady, whose whims you will cater to with charm and graciousness. You'll be her escort, ply her with compliments and affection, and if she wishes it, you will bed her."

Edward flinched, staring into Benedict's cold blue eyes and finding that the man seemed to be completely serious. He looked to Hugh, who also showed no outward indication that this was some kind of joke. But, obviously they were having him on, because Edward had never heard such a ridiculous thing in his life.

He smirked, the motion of his lips soon spreading into a full-fledged grin. Then, his shoulders began to tremble and the snorts he tried to smother turned into uproarious chuckles. His eyes watered as he slapped his thigh with one hand. His chest ached from how hard it became to draw breath, laughter spilling from him uncontrolled.

"Oh, God!" he guffawed. "I haven't had my leg pulled like that in ages. And look at the two of you ... so serious, as if you actually meant it. I say, bloody good one, Hugh!"

He expected that at any moment, the other two men would drop the act and laugh along with him, wiping moisture away from their eyes before finally telling him what he'd really be doing. Yet, after several seconds it became clear this wouldn't be the case. Realizing he was the only one laughing, and that Benedict now looked annoyed while Hugh seemed embarrassed, Edward fell silent. The sober realization that they really *had* been serious washed over him like a tidal wave.

He sprang to his feet. "God's blood, you're serious!"

"As the grave," Benedict replied with a roll of his eyes. "The Gentleman Courtesans has been in business for a year, quite successfully I might add."

Edward turned to Hugh, who gave him a sheepish smile. "I warned you that it was scandalous. But, the business is lucrative and all it costs is hours of your time a few nights a week."

"It's no more than you might do for free," Benedict offered with a raised eyebrow. "Whatever your money troubles are, consider them over once I've arranged for you to have your first keeper. And if she's made happy enough, you won't need a new arrangement for quite some time."

When Benedict put it that way, there really was nothing Edward could say in protest. He hadn't been with a woman in months, his father's death and the resulting problems it had caused taking up most of his time. That he'd now get paid to bed a lady ought to leave a bitter taste in his mouth, yet somehow it did not. Men paid for the use of mistresses all the time, and the women in such situations were well provided for. As he thought of Jacob and Caroline, who were counting on him to settle the family's affairs, and the business that threatened to drag them all down, Edward realized he had no choice. It wasn't as if any other promising offers had fallen into his lap. Even with the burden of the family business on his shoulders, he had attempted to find proper employment—something he was qualified to do that would provide the needed funds. However, his efforts had seen him faced with rejection and a heightened sense of desperation that grew worse by the day.

Entertaining a wealthy woman in and out of bed sounded far preferable to debtor's prison or watching Caroline be forced to work her fingers to the bone to support herself. As the head of his family, it fell to him to ensure that everyone was provided for, and this opportunity was the best he was likely to receive.

Edward had no expectations for himself in terms of a marriage or courting a proper lady given the state of his finances, but he would need to ensure that his new occupation did not cause any further embarrassment to his family's reputation and standing.

Glancing about Hugh's drawing room, he pictured himself living in such comfort. He imagined gracing Caroline with the sort of dowry that would see her married well, and perhaps even financing a Grand Tour for Jacob. He'd fuck a hundred ladies if that was what it took to make those imaginings into reality.

Turning to Benedict, Edward smiled. "I'm in."

CHAPTER 1

LONDON, TWO WEEKS LATER ...

Throwing open the door to the study adjoining her bedchamber, Clare Dunnaby heaved a sigh of relief. A servant had thought to start a fire in the hearth in preparation for her arrival home, and it went a long way toward warding off the chill clinging to her. It had been a miserably cold and foggy morning, but she'd been looking forward to inspecting the newest exhibits at the British Museum for weeks now. Rain and cold be damned, Clare had been determined not to suffer from boredom while cloistered away indoors. Tenacity was her middle name, and she was often known for going against all prudence when it came to whatever she wanted most at the moment.

Actually, Cecelia was her middle name, but had she been able to choose her own middle name, she would have chosen Tenacity. Armored with resolve to enjoy her outing—along with a pelisse that buttoned to the throat and a cumbersome umbrella—she'd taken the walk from Bedford Square to the museum. Such weather was good for a hearty constitution, her aunt always told her, but while Clare often found light summer showers enjoyable, today's inclement conditions left much to be desired. She peeled off her gloves while striding closer to the fire, tossing them aside without bothering to notice how they fell.

The housekeeper would swoon in a dead faint if she trod into Clare's private domain, but Aunt Helene ordered the servants to keep out. The room had been transformed into a study of sorts, filled with tables, desks, and shelves which contained the assortment of items related to Clare's intellectual interests. She was unforgivably absent-minded and, as Aunt Helene affectionately called her, an irredeemable sloven. It wasn't that she enjoyed making additional work for the chambermaids, or even that she had no care for her belongings. It was simply that her mind never ceased working long enough for her to give thought to anything beyond whatever held her attention.

And, at the moment, the thing capturing her interest was the parcel lying on her writing desk. It had been delivered during her outing, and the moment sensation returned to her numb fingers she would tear it open. She'd been waiting for the parcel for months now, and could hardly contain her excitement over what might be inside.

While the heat of the fire seeped through the layers of her clothes, she set to work making herself comfortable. Fumbling with the buttons of her pelisse, she peeled the damp garment off and flung it in the direction of the coat tree in the corner of the room. It fell into a heap, just missing its target and landing amongst a cloak and a spencer she'd forgotten to pick up and return to her lady's maid for cleaning. Untying the ribbons of her bonnet, she tried again for the coat tree, smiling as she made her mark, sending the headwear spinning before it settled on its perch.

Her fingers no longer feeling like rigid icicles, Clare went to her desk while running them through hair cropped to chin length. In her youth, the locks had fallen to her waist in a heavy tumble of glossy black waves. However, she no longer had the patience to sit while her maid combed, brushed, and styled it. Clare found that the shortened hair freed up much of her time for more important things—such as her study of botany, her collections, and her books.

Before settling into her chair, she located the bell-pull and rang, desirous of a hot drink and something to nibble on as she whiled away the hours before dinner in her study. That done, she reached for her parcel, barely able to contain a wide grin as she tore through the brown paper. Inside, she found a plain box with a folded and sealed letter resting on top. Despite wanting to get to the contents of the box, she opened the letter first. Upon the stationary inside, she found the familiar handwriting of her dear friend, Gillian Young.

Dearest CeCe,

Do forgive me for taking so long to write. Our arrival in Cornwall preceded a whirlwind of activity as we settled in with Randall's associates. Then, the excavation began and my daylight hours have been spent at toiling and discovery. The weather has impeded our work some days, but the moment the soil is dry enough we go right back to our site and resume our work. We've unearthed quite a few interesting specimens, a few of which I have enclosed samples of for your collection.

I do apologize for the shortness of this letter, but am certain you understand. We've only a few days left before we begin our travels again, and I hope our next destination proves as diverting as this one has been.

Thank you so much for including the pressed blossoms with your last letter. The cluster of Delphinium gypsophilum Ewan was my favorite. I look forward to your next letter, though it might be best for you to withhold it until I can apprise you of where we will travel to next, along with the address.

Randall sends his warmest regards.

Your friend,

Gilly

P.S. - on the back of this letter you will find a list of the specimens I sent for your collection.

Setting the letter aside, Clare slid the box closer to her and paused, allowing the anticipation to build before she would permit herself the satisfaction of knowing what lay within. She tried not to think on the inclusion of Randall's greeting in Gillian's letter. Her friend's elder brother had expressed an interest in her a year ago, before the siblings had embarked on their journey of geological exploration. He had even invited her to join them, likely in an attempt to appeal to her intellectual tendencies, knowing he had little chance of appealing to her romantic ones.

It wasn't that she had no interest in the opposite sex, only that she'd had yet to find a man who could capture her attention as easily as a good book, a scientific essay, or her beloved plants. She found it ever so ironic that one of the only men not repelled by her pursuits—on the contrary, he seemed drawn to her *because* of them—and Clare felt absolutely nothing but sibling-like kinship toward him. She and Gillian had been friends for so long, the other woman felt like the sister she'd always wanted, making Randall more like a brother to her than anything else. She only wished the man would finally realize this and turn his attentions elsewhere.

She'd turned down the invitation, for she would not leave Aunt Helene alone for the world. Besides that, she had also hoped time and distance would turn Randall's attentions away from her and toward some other woman—one who would feel affection for him in return. It would seem that was not yet the case.

Shrugging aside those thoughts, she slowly opened the box, her breath catching at the sight of the specimens laid inside. The door to her study opened and footsteps approached, but she couldn't be bothered to look up as a maid set a tray of tea and biscuits atop the stack of books resting on one corner of the desk. No one needed to ask why she'd rung, for all the servants knew that a summons from her study meant someone was to bring her tea and then promptly exit without disturbing her. The maid did that now, leaving her to contemplate the collection in peace.

She absently nibbled on a biscuit while taking up each stone and comparing them to Gillian's list. There was a triangular hunk of beige and black speckled cassiterite in quartz, a small jade green slab of iridescent quartz, a jagged bit of cuprite sporting swirls of aquamarine and deep red, and a multifaceted piece of sky-blue chalcedony.

Forgetting about her refreshment, she fumbled about the clutter of her desk until locating her magnifying glass, needing more than the assistance of her brass-rimmed spectacles to properly study the stones.

Lifting the cuprite until its surface gleamed in the light of the taper resting nearby, she peered at it through the glass. She was so engrossed by the contrasting swirls of aquamarine and red that she hardly heard the knock upon her door. Without bothering to answer it, she turned the stone over in her hand and studied it from a different angle. The door swung open despite her refusal to urge the person to enter, and she didn't bother to look up—knowing that after tea had been delivered, only one person would dare enter her domain without permission.

Aunt Helene's familiar rose-oil scent wafted up her nostrils the moment before she spied the woman in her periphery.

"Aunt," she murmured, laying the cuprite back into the box and selecting the chalcedony.

"CeCe, dear ... how was your trip to the museum?" her aunt asked, leaning against the corner of her desk.

"Quite diverting, and far preferable to spending all day trapped indoors. What have you been up to today?"

"Why, preparing to surprise you for your birthday, of course."

Clare paused, the stone falling from her fingers and into the box with a 'thunk'. At last, she peered up at Helene, who gave her a smug smile, her bright blue eyes twinkling with mirth. Even as she approached her sixtieth year, her aunt proved to be a stunning woman. Smile lines around her eyes and a few wrinkles only added character to a remarkable face. To the everlasting despair of every eligible man of a certain age in London, Helene was adamant that she would never marry again after being widowed. Clare had always doted upon her aunt, seeing her as a model of the sort of woman she wanted to be. Independent, intelligent, and unconcerned with the thoughts and opinions of others.

"My birthday?" she murmured, furrowing her brow. "My ..."

Helene pilfered a biscuit from Clare's tray and took a dainty bite. "It is April 25th, my dear. The day of your birth, you might recall."

Clare's frown deepened as she sat up straighter in her chair. "No, that cannot be right. It can't be so late in the month already."

"Of course it is," Helene insisted. "You've lost track of time again, busy as you have been with your plants and your rocks and such."

"Minerals," she corrected. "Or, specimens as Gillian calls them."

"Oh, you've heard from Gilly. I do love that dear girl. How is she?"

Clare lifted her letter from the desk and waved it through the air. "Enjoying Cornwall and already plotting her next destination. But, back to the matter at hand. Are you *certain* it is my birthday? Perhaps you are the one who has the date wrong."

Helene rolled her eyes and took another bite of her biscuit. "Today's copy of the *Post* begs to differ. It is your birthday, my dear, and I've planned something especially wonderful for you this year."

Raising her eyebrows, Clare found herself intrigued. "More wonderful than that hot air balloon ride last year? I was so grateful you convinced Mr. Kent to allow us to come along for his ascent. A most bracing experience!"

"Even better than that," Helene declared. "It is not every day a girl turns one-and-twenty after all."

Clare shrugged. "One would think receiving my inheritance would be gift enough."

"That gift is from your parents, God rest them," Helene replied, her expression growing wistful for a moment before she smiled. "This is something special, from me."

Every birthday saw her on the receiving end of an extravagant gift from Helene, her aunt's way of making the occasion special for her. It had been this way since she and her sister, Alice, had come to live with Helene after the deaths of both their parents. Having never borne children of her own, Helene had leaped in with both feet to raise two young girls alone. It was Clare's opinion that she'd done an admirable job of it, even if Alice had departed from them to marry a baron years ago without a look back. Her elder sister proved as different from Helene and Clare as a bird from a fish. While Alice seemed to have been made for the shallow social world of the *ton*, Helene and Clare were content to live on the edge of it while making their own rules. They had no care for propriety or social norms, while Alice lived her life by them to a rigid degree.

This was why Clare could never have gone off to Cornwall to leave Helene alone in London. Her aunt had a busy social life as well as her own circle of friends to spend her time with. However, though she tried to hide it, Clare could see it hurt her aunt that Alice seemed to want nothing to do with either of them. She enjoyed her younger niece's presence in her home, and Clare liked the freedom as well as the companionship of remaining in the same home with one of the few people in the world who understood her. Besides, if she left, who would make such a grand affair of her birthday each year, even when she forgot about it herself?

Setting her magnifying glass aside, Clare rose and smoothed her skirts. "Well then, where is this gift? I find I am most anxious to know what it is, even though I did not realize it was my birthday until a few seconds ago."

A wide, catlike grin spread across her aunt's face, and the woman stood from her perch on the corner of the desk. Motioning toward the connecting door to Clare's bedchamber, her eyes glittered with excitement and mischief.

"I've stashed it in your bedroom, dear. I do hope you enjoy it."

Without waiting for further explanation—and knowing her aunt had a flare for the dramatic—Clare went to the door. Throwing it open, she noticed that a fire and several tapers had been lit within. Stepping farther into the chamber she found that nothing seemed out of the ordinary. She'd half expected to discover that her aunt had wedged an entire circus inside her room, complete with acrobats, jugglers, and elephants. One might argue that the elephants would never fit, but her aunt was nothing if not resourceful. Baby elephants, perhaps.

However, she saw nothing other than the usual order maintained by her lady's maid. Helene hadn't redecorated, as there had been no change to the chinese wallpaper, heavy oak furniture, or silk seafoam green curtains.

Glancing over her shoulder at the closed door, she wondered if she ought to go ask Helene if she had hidden the gift. Perhaps Clare was meant to hunt for it.

But then, the rustle of fabric caught her attention and had her whirling to face the bed. Her mouth fell open as amongst the tousled mess of her unmade bedclothes, she found the very last thing she would have expected.

A man who appeared to be stark naked.

Good heavens, there's a nude man in my bed! Her stomach performed a somersault as she noticed that he was quite an intriguing specimen of manhood—light brown hair falling in an artful tumble about his head, refined, angular features, and an upper body that suggested strength and agility. She'd seen a man unclothed before, but had not found him as pleasant to look upon as this one, with sinewy lines and bulges of muscles stretching along his chest and arms.

As he sat up in bed and met her gaze, a slow, sensual smile transformed his face into something sinful. It *must* be a sin for someone to look so delectably carnal—all full lips, mussed hair, and smooth, bare skin. Staring at him without blinking, she noticed that his eyes were a lovely shade of deep jade, akin to the chunk of quartz in the next room.

Her mouth went dry when those perfect lips of his parted to form words, emitting a deep, pleasing baritone.

"Hello, Clare."

CHAPTER 2

Helene Dunnaby had told Edward that her niece was beautiful, but Edward hadn't placed much stock in that claim. Of course the woman thought her niece was beautiful; she was practically obligated to believe that. However, as he lay in Clare's bed taking her in from head to toe, he realized that Helene had grossly understated the allure of the creature standing before him.

While not pretty by the conventions of the *ton*, she possessed the sort of features that demanded closer inspection. Individually, her features might not have seemed so remarkable, but together they made a riveting picture. Hair dark as midnight fell in soft waves to her chin, cut in a style he saw on few women but that suited her perfectly. Matching brows arched over bright, expressive blue eyes, which at the moment conveyed both her shock and curiosity. A heavy fringe of sooty lashes made them seem unusually bright and electric, almost as if a painter had applied the most vivid of his blue pigments over her irises. Sloping cheekbones gave her face a sharp sort of structure, while a wide lush mouth promised an exuberant smile. The slightest of dimples accentuated her chin, like a punctuation mark completing the whole of her visage.

Her gown draped what appeared to be a willowy frame, complete with long legs he suddenly wanted wrapped around his waist.

While Benedict had informed him that he had no control over the comeliness of his first keeper, Edward had been prepared to do his duty. After all, this particular arrangement paid especially well and his desperation for funds was as acute as ever. But, looking upon Clare, he decided that he'd have gladly bedded the chit for free.

One hand pressed against her chest, and the more she stared at him the wider her lovely eyes got. Helene had hired him as a surprise for her niece, paying an exorbitant amount for him to act as the girl's lover for a month. It would seem the element of surprise had been achieved, but Edward could not yet tell if Clare were pleased by it.

"Hello, Clare," he murmured.

His voice seemed to shock her out of her stupor.

"Who are you, and what are you doing in my bed?"

The sharp, commanding voice that fell from her mouth took him by complete surprise—though not in a particularly negative way. She sounded like a governess scolding a naughty pupil. He couldn't puzzle out why that made his cock twitch beneath the coverlet.

"I'm Edward," he told her. "And I am in your bed because your aunt invited me to await you here ... Happy Birthday, by the way."

She raised her eyebrows, staring at him in clear disbelief. She fell silent, and he could see her trying to work things out in her mind, to arrive at the inevitable conclusion. He hadn't thought Helene would send Clare in blind, but apparently the young woman had been left to draw the right inference before taking advantage of his unclothed body.

At last, she seemed to snap out of it, though instead of rushing to the bed to join him she burst out laughing. He could hardly dwell on how pleasantly boisterous the sound was—loud, clear, and downright heartwarming—when he was overwhelmed by a swift surge of embarrassment. The last thing a man wanted to hear while naked in a woman's bed was laughter.

"Oh ... oh, that is so *funny*," she guffawed, doubling over as her shoulders trembled with mirth. "Aunt Helene is such a trickster. She would truly have me believe that *you* are supposed to be my birthday gift, and … and I'm supposed to … oh, it's too hilarious!"

Edward scowled as she went on laughing, though he couldn't help but notice that he'd been right to assume she'd have a stunning smile. That mouth might have seemed too wide on another woman, overtaking her entire aspect, but on this woman it was perfection. Still, he'd rather not be on the receiving end of her amusement.

Throwing back the coverlet, he rose from the bed and approached, his jaw clenched. She gasped, her laughter fading to silence as she raked her gaze over his body. She took stock of his chest and abdomen, pausing for a long moment at the jut of his cock—which had begun to rise to attention the moment he'd laid eyes on her—down his legs, then back to his face. Her cheeks took on a becoming pink blush, and she made a sound low in her throat that might be interpreted as one of approval.

"Well, there is nothing funny about *that*," she murmured. "I thank you for going along with my aunt's prank, Mr...."

"Edward," he reminded her, crossing his arms over his chest.

"Right, Edward. It has been lovely meeting you, and truly...you are quite a...fascinating specimen of a man. But whatever my real gift is, perhaps you might tell me where to find it. Or has my aunt instructed me to guess? Oh, maybe it is in the dressing room."

He swiftly moved to impede her path, her long legs carrying her right against him.

"Oh!" she exclaimed when she stumbled, hands pressed to his bare chest as she fought to stay on her feet.

He took hold of her arms to steady her, then drew her even closer, until every inch of her was pressed against him. She stared at him with parted lips, her breath hitching with a noisy inhale. Desire knifed through him, sharp and hot, filling him with the need to taste her, undress her, lay her down on the bed and turn her laughter into moans of pleasure.

"I can assure you, this is no prank," he rasped, leaning in until all he could see were the brilliant orbs of her eyes, which were rimmed with a darker blue along the edges. "I am yours for however long you wish it."

Her reply was muffled against his mouth as he closed the distance between them to steal a kiss. Whatever she'd been about to say melted into a surprised gasp, which then rose to a startled moan of delight. Bracing his hands at her upper back, he held her tight enough to show her he meant business, but loose enough that she could escape him if she wished. She seemed to have no such desire, her lips going pliant and then returning his ardent pressure with her own searching kiss.

His cock grew hard as a brick in an instant, pressing insistently against her. She arched into him, opening her mouth for the demanding sweep of his tongue against the seam of her lips. He groaned at the taste of her, sweet from some confection she'd recently eaten, as well as a bit earthy as if she'd just sipped tea. Her scent invaded his senses, a mixture of lavender and rosemary. Her body, which seemed comprised of all straight lines from a distance, proved soft and womanly with slight curves up close, the small, high mounds of her breasts pressed tight against his chest, the flare of her hips filling his hands as he trailed them down to explore her further.

The kiss ended as suddenly as it began when she wrenched her mouth free of his with a gasp. Retreating from him as if he'd burned her, she stared at him with wide eyes. Her fingers came up to her lips, which were reddened and slightly swollen from his kiss. She was even more alluring with desire glazing her eyes and her breasts heaving with strained breath, that decadent mouth begging for more kisses.

He didn't think he'd ever wanted to fuck a woman more than he did right at that moment.

"Dear God," Clare mumbled, shaking her head as if to clear it. "She really did ... I cannot believe ... *Aunt Helene!*"

Edward started when her voice raised in pitch and volume, echoing off the walls of the chamber. Within seconds, Helene appeared with an amused smirk curving her lips.

"Goodness, I had expected to hear Edward's name screamed to the rooftops of this house, not mine," she quipped. Then, she noticed him standing there in the buff, and gave him a once-over much the way her niece had. "Oh my ... very nice, Mr. Norton."

Deciding he was in no mood to stand about naked while aunt and niece had it out, he snatched the coverlet from the bed and wrapped it around his waist.

"What is the meaning of this?" Clare asked, sweeping a hand in his general direction.

She did not sound angry, simply a bit confused. Perhaps Clare was a virgin who had no notion of what to do with a naked man. Had she not ended their kiss, he would have been more than happy to show her.

"Darling, I didn't think I'd have to *explain* my gift. I think it should be obvious."

Clare made an exasperated sound, looking as if she'd very much like to strangle her aunt. "Of course it is obvious. What I mean to ask is, what on earth would lead you to believe I'd even want such a gift? And how did you even convince this man to go along with such a plan?"

Edward swiveled his gaze back and forth as he followed the exchange between the two women, finding himself completely absorbed by it. He'd known their relationship must be unconventional —after all, how many aunts would think nothing of hiring a courtesan to service their nieces? And for Clare to have not even batted an eyelash at the sight of his unclothed body suggested she was as worldly and unconventional as her aunt.

"The same way I convinced Mr. Kent to take you up in his balloon, of course. With money."

Clare gaped at him for a moment before turning to glare at her aunt. "Do you mean to tell me that this man is a ... a whore?"

Her aunt sniffed. "Of course not, dear. I'd never be so uncouth. He's a courtesan."

Now it was Edward's turn to be amused as Clare took on an expression of complete and utter dismay.

"A *courtesan*? Whoever heard of a *male* courtesan?"

"Well, I have, obviously," Helene retorted. "And now so have you. I thought you would be happy, darling. You bury yourself in your intellectual pursuits, and while I know you love them I thought a bit of diversion might—"

"Might what?" Clare interjected. "Inject some much-needed excitement into my boring spinster life?"

Helene frowned, taking a step toward her niece. "Of course not. And you're hardly old enough to be considered a spinster just yet."

The woman's words fell on deaf ears as Clare marched over to where he'd left his clothing piled in a chair. "I will have you know that if I want a bedmate, I can very well go out and find one of my own. I have before, you know."

Edward raised his brows at that. So, Clare wasn't a shy virgin as he'd first assumed. She'd simply been caught off guard, and had recovered enough to rain hellfire down on them with her sharp tongue.

Intriguing.

Clare approached him now, extending his garments to him and giving him a pitying glance. "I am certain you are a very good...I mean, I'm sure you are only doing what you were paid for. But, your services won't be needed. Please, get dressed. I apologize for any misunderstanding."

"CeCe, wait," Helene called out, rushing to follow Clare as she made long strides toward the door.

Edward fumbled with his breeches while the aunt's eyes were averted, a sick feeling overwhelming him. His first day as a courtesan, and he was already an abysmal failure. However, Benedict had never told him how he ought to handle such a situation. But then, all this must be highly irregular. He would be willing to bet he was the only one of the Gentleman Courtesans who'd ever been hired as an unwanted gift for someone. With a muttered curse he pulled his shirt on.

Clare exited the room without a look back, while Helene stared at the open doorway with a frown.

"Well, that certainly did not go the way I'd anticipated," she murmured before turning to face him, a determined expression settling on her face. "Mr. Norton, I am so sorry about this. I can see that my surprise has fallen flat. Oh well, there's nothing to it but for us to try again."

He paused with one arm through his waistcoat, giving Helene a dubious look. She couldn't be serious. If Clare didn't want his services, he didn't know what Helene intended to do about it. Then again, he didn't want to think about what ending his first arrangement before it had begun would mean. The rather obscene sum she'd paid Benedict would have to be returned before either of them had taken their share. Perhaps the leader of the Gentleman Courtesans would then decide Edward hadn't been worth hiring. He'd failed before he'd truly begun.

"I beg your pardon?" he asked.

Helene shrugged one shoulder, then waved a hand in the direction Clare had taken. "My niece wasn't immune to you. I could see that much when I walked into this room. Tell me...before she called out to me, did anything happen between the two of you?"

He scoffed while fastening the buttons of his waistcoat. "Well, when I informed her why I was here, she laughed."

His ears burned as he shoved one foot into a stocking, remembering the humiliation of her laughter. Oh, but then...

"What happened next?" Helene prodded.

"I convinced her that it most certainly was not a joke by kissing her."

Helene grinned, her eyes alighting with hope. "And how was it?"

He paused before going for his shoes, equal parts discomfort and arousal flooding him in a rush. It wasn't seemly for him to allow thoughts of that electrifying kiss to overtake his senses while Clare's aunt stood before him. If he dwelt on it for too long, proof of just how good the kiss had been would show itself at the front of his breeches. However, he did realize that Helene was right. Clare certainly wasn't indifferent to him, and her response to his kiss had proven that. He'd been seconds away from tempting her into that bed with him before she'd pulled away.

"She enjoyed it," he said. "I think perhaps she did not want to...but she did."

Helene rubbed her hands together. "Good. This is good. It is as I said, you must try again. Now that she knows what you are, she won't be so surprised next time you meet. I know Clare. Once she has had some time to cool off, she will come to her senses."

Edward studied Helene for a long moment before speaking, trying without success to make sense of all this. "Begging your pardon, but it doesn't seem as if she's interested. Would it not be simpler to ask Ben for your money back and count it as a loss?"

Helene gave him a little smile. "I never give up, Mr. Norton. Besides, I do not think it would do you or your agency much good to be forced to return my money, and I'd rather not have to ask that of you. Am I mistaken in assuming you need the funds?"

Running a hand through his hair, he thought back to his sister and her excitement over the impending change in their fortune. It would break her heart to learn that he would be unable to deliver on his promises, and it would ruin them all for Norton & Rivers to fail to recover.

"Desperately," he admitted. "But that is not your problem. It's mine."

"It may not be, but I don't relish sending you away and accepting defeat," she argued. "Please, won't you try one more time? Let me talk to her and smooth the way, then you may return tomorrow. I promise you will find her far more amenable."

Edward wanted to press her for answers and discover just why this was so important to Helene. Most aunts would want their nieces seeking a husband, not a courtesan, and remain chaste in the process. But he'd understood that theirs was an irregular relationship from the start. And truly, it was none of his affair. If Clare could be convinced to give him a chance, it would solve all his problems for the time being. The amount he stood to gain in this arrangement would be enough to pay the debts of Norton & Rivers, update Caroline's wardrobe, pay his staff for a few months, and ensure they had more to eat than chicken, bread, and eggs. With the debts paid for the business, he could then move forward with ship repairs and open the line for business once again. Within half a year they'd earn enough to turn a profit. Should his time with Clare end before he felt comfortable with the business's state of affairs, he'd simply seek another keeper, and another, until he no longer felt the need to go on doing this.

But, of course, for all that to happen he needed Clare to accept him into her life and her bed. He couldn't give Benedict cause to cut him loose, and he didn't have another fortnight to wait for a new keeper to be found for him.

Devil take it. This had to work, for he truly could afford no other option now, not when the business was on the very edge of collapsing forever.

"Very well," he relented, finishing off the knot in his cravat. "I will return tomorrow afternoon, but if Clare still doesn't want this, I will not press the issue."

Helene beamed at him. "Thank you for being so understanding. I know this situation isn't typical, but I promise it will be worth your while."

As he followed Helene downstairs, Edward realized there was one other reason he'd let her convince him to try again. Aside from needing the funds, he found himself unable to forget the sight of Clare —eyes round with shock, then twinkling with amusement before melting into vibrant blue pools of desire. The feel of her body against him, the taste of her, the little sounds she'd made when their tongues had met. He wanted her, badly. More than he ought to since he'd only known her for a few minutes. He'd likely go to bed tonight with a hard cock and a mind overwhelming him with thoughts of what might have happened had she not ended their kiss.

Yes, he would return, and he would employ every weapon in his seductive arsenal until she gave in.

Edward left Helene's townhouse with a smirk curving his lips as he thought over the pleasures to come in Clare's bed. If a man had to sell himself for coin, he might as well do it with a woman as desirable as her.

CHAPTER 3

Clare slammed the clay pot on the wooden surface of her worktable, rattling the various implements she used in her study of plants. Her movements were abrupt as she shoveled soil into the pot, her teeth gritted so hard it made her jaw ache.

Typically, she found peace and happiness inside the small greenhouse filling the back courtyard, but today her anger and annoyance had followed her. She glowered at her collection of plants—some fully bloomed and others in various states of growth. The accomplishments of her various crossbreeding experiments paled in comparison to her embarrassment over what had just occurred in her bedroom. What had been meant as a gift hadn't made her very happy. Instead, it only reminded Clare of her one and only experience with intercourse, an altogether uninteresting affair lasting a single night. Upon telling Aunt Helene about the forgettable encounter, she'd sworn off romantic relationships with men altogether. Why subject herself to the sweating, groaning attentions of anyone else if she would simply lie there in puzzled disappointment afterward?

In the years since then, she'd found joy in her work in the greenhouse, managing her various collections, and deepening her friendships with other like-minded intellectuals of both genders. While more than a few men had made their interest known, Clare had always rebuffed them as kindly as possible, keeping all her relationships with the opposite sex on a strictly platonic level.

Despite having been told that love and desire were powerful, all-consuming forces, she had never experienced them for herself. Even while finding a few men of her acquaintance attractive, she'd never been seized with the urge to form an attachment to one—physical or otherwise. Because of this, dreams of a husband and children had been pushed aside in favor of her other pursuits. If there was no man to be found who could make her want it with all her heart, then Clare saw no reason to bind herself to anyone for the rest of her life. She wanted it all—the love, the happiness, the desire—or she wanted none of it. She was content with life as it was, being an heiress in pursuit of her hobbies and intellectual diversions.

Using her gloved fingers to create a well in the soil for her seeds, she scoffed in disbelief. Just what had her aunt thought to accomplish with this little stunt? Clare had assumed Helene had given up after her insistence that it wouldn't always be like her first time had fallen on deaf ears. Aunt Helene had engaged in her own discreet affairs over the years, so she certainly had more experience to draw on than Clare. That didn't make her eager to go diving into the beds of every man who paid her attention in hopes that one of them would prove better than the first. It hardly seemed worth the time, and she had better things to do; such as potting her hybrid seeds and cross-pollinating another set of parent plants to make a fresh batch.

She covered her seeds with soil using far more force than was necessary, but she had no other outlet for her frustration. Peeling off one of her work gloves, she scratched out a note in her journal. The lead of her pencil grated against the paper with swift strokes as she recorded the date she'd planted the seeds born of cross-pollination between the *candidum* and *superbum* species of *Lilium*.

The results of her other hybrid experiments sat strewn on every available space beneath the glass ceiling—blood red lilies with orange centers, others boasting purple petals bleeding toward white tips, and her personal favorite, a brilliant overgrowth of blossoms flaunting magenta petals melting into sunny yellow. The *Lilium superbum* seeds had been a gift from the wife of an American botanist she'd befriended years ago. The foreign plant had thrived in the moist, humid environment of her greenhouse, and now she could discover whether the brilliant colors of the Turk's cap lily would burst through with the shape and hardiness of the Madonna lily.

She'd just set the first pot aside and reached for another when the door opened and Aunt Helene appeared before her, brows knit with concern. Giving her aunt a glare, she then went back to her work, filling this pot with as much aggression as she had the first.

"I can see you are still angry with me," Helene declared, watching Clare shovel the soil as if burying a dead body instead of seeds. "You usually handle your plants with more care."

"Seeds are hardy," Clare argued without looking up. "They are in no danger of suffering at my hands."

Helene leaned closer, filling the periphery of her vision. "And what of misguided, contrite aunts?"

Pausing with spade in hand, she flicked an irritated gaze at her aunt. "Contrite, you?"

Helene chuckled when Clare issued a rough snort, then pulled a stool closer to the table before sinking onto it. Hands braced on the table, she turned her head to admire the Turk's cap.

"Perhaps not contrite about my motives," she admitted. "But the way I went about springing it on you...I suppose it wasn't very well done."

"It certainly was not," Clare agreed, carefully extracting more seeds from the small ceramic pot she'd stored them in. "Though I question your motives as well as the execution of your little *gift*."

"Is it so wrong of me to want more for you, Clare?"

Slamming her spade down and finally meeting her aunt's gaze, she shook her head. "More than what? A life I chose and enjoy just the way it is? You've always allowed me my independence, and I am grateful for that. At what point did that independence end? When you decided it is time for me to take a lover?"

Helene squared her shoulders, displaying the same stubbornness

Clare had learned directly from her. "I have also gone out of my way to open your eyes to the boundless experiences of the world: travel, cuisine, art, intellectual pursuits—"

"I see," Clare spat. "Now that the others have been accomplished, intercourse must be next on your list of experiences."

Raising an eyebrow, her aunt gave her a knowing look. "I didn't have to introduce you to that particular experience, did I? You went out and discovered it on your own. Intercourse isn't what I was referring to, CeCe. Pleasure...that is the experience I was speaking of."

Despite not being an ignorant maiden, Clare's face flushed hot and she broke Helene's gaze. "That word and its connotation are purely subjective. I derive pleasure from my collections, from working in this greenhouse, from meeting and getting to know scholars and artists and the sorts of people who stimulate my mind."

"My dear, your mind is merely one part of you. Do you want to die an old, shriveled up woman who's never known what it's like to want someone to the point of madness? Trust me, there are enough of those amongst the ranks of the *ton*, and you do not want to be one of them."

Clare crossed her arms over her chest. "Is that how you see me—as some sort of hopeless case in need of charity?"

Helene sighed, clearly exasperated, and seemed to try to remain calm in the face of Clare's anger. "Of course not. I just did not want your first experience to make you believe it isn't worth trying again with someone else. Someone discreet, whose only aim is to please you. Who you can try it with as many times and in as many ways as you wish until you've decided what you like and what you don't like. Why, in truth, it sounds rather a lot like your hybrid experiments!"

Furrowing her brow, she studied her aunt for signs of insanity. "That is the most ridiculous thing I've ever heard you say."

Rising to her feet, Helene grinned. "Hear me out, CeCe. In this greenhouse, you take this white lily."

"*Lilium candidum*," Clare grumbled, unable to let go of her habit of reminding her aunt of the scientific terms for the plants.

"Right," Helene relented. "You take this *Lilium candidum*, and mate it with this...this..."

"*Lilium superbum.*"

"Yes, such a pretty plant, by the way. You mate them several times and in different ways in order to discover the outcome of what they can create together. What these two plants produce will not come out the same as what you make if you were to cross this same *Lilium candidum* with this."

Clare scowled as her aunt pointed toward an entirely different plant. "*Lilium henyri,*" she offered grudgingly.

Helene nodded her thanks, and pressed on. "At times, you might experiment with plants that produce an undesirable outcome. But, do you give up on the process entirely? Of course not! You simply move forward and find your *Lilium candidum* a new match...one that will produce the most vibrant flowers you've ever seen."

As her aunt's words sank in, Clare could not help but admit they had the ring of truth to them. Her one-night affair had been just as Helene described—an experiment to appease her curiosity. Displeased with the results, she had decided it was not worth pursuing again, with the same man or with anyone else.

Now that her initial anger had faded and she'd decided to forgive Helene for the artless presentation of her gift, Clare supposed she could see that her aunt meant well. Her motives had certainly been pure, even if a bit odd. But then, their relationship had never been like that of normal mothers and daughters, even though this woman had raised her. She'd never made Clare feel ashamed of her inquisitive mind, and had answered every question she'd ever posed with blunt honesty. Of course she would think it acceptable for her to introduce Clare to a male courtesan.

With a sigh, she peered at Helene over the rim of her spectacles. "You might have explained it that way before sending me into that room, you know."

Helene threw her head back and laughed, the boisterous sound echoing through the small space. "As I said, my methods might have been ill-judged but I regret nothing. I simply cannot allow you to quit after only one go. Edward is receiving an exorbitant sum to be at your beck and call. Aside from that, he appeared quite...virile. More so than that Barnaby."

Clare snickered. "His name was Baldwin."

Wrinkling her brow, Helene shook her head slowly. "No...I am almost certain his name was Barnaby. Don't try to make me feel old, my mind is a steel trap—I never forget a name or a face."

"Are you certain about that?" Clare teased.

"Of course I am," Helene insisted. "Perhaps *you* have forgotten—your mind's way of removing such an unpleasant memory. So you've forgotten his name as well. It was Barnaby, by the way."

"God, you might just be right," Clare murmured. "Baldwin Barnaby was the most forgettable man I've ever had the misfortune of knowing. He had a weak chin and even weaker hands."

She cringed at the memory of those hands on her, and swiftly pushed it from her thoughts. If she dwelt on that for too long, she'd find herself retreating from this idea even swifter than before.

"Edward certainly didn't look as if he had weak hands."

He didn't, and Clare could now attest to that. There was nothing weak or off-putting about him, something that became easier to accept now that her ire had cooled. The press of his body against hers had been hard, warm, and masculine, such a contrast to her own form in a way she'd never given thought to, even when lying with Baldwin Barnaby. Edward had kissed her with a commanding finesse, making her lose complete hold of her senses with nothing more than the touch of his mouth. Oh, but she couldn't forget the hands now that her aunt had brought them up. His touch had sent electricity arcing over her skin, and an achy tightness to the tips of her breasts.

It had all happened so fast, she hadn't been able to discern just what that heady, confusing feeling had been until now.

Desire. Edward had stoked passion in her with nothing but a kiss, something her first lover had failed to do while lying naked between her spread legs.

"CeCe?" Helene prodded when she failed to respond. "Are you all right? Thinking of Edward's hands?"

She met her aunt's wicked grin with a slow nod, though her mind took her far beyond that suggest.

Yes, I am thinking of his hands...and his mouth...and that ridiculously perfect body. And his cock.

She gave her head a swift shake before her thoughts took her any farther down that road. Entertaining the idea was all well and good, but she couldn't lose her head over it. If she decided to go through with it, she would approach it just as her aunt had suggested: as an intellectual experiment. She would attempt intercourse with Edward as many times as it took for her to decide whether she was capable of the sort of fiery passion her aunt described, or whether a kiss would be the most she could ever enjoy. No other man had managed to bring such curiosity to the surface again, and now that Edward had, Clare was gripped with the need to explore further. It didn't have to get in the way of her life if she did not let it. Nothing had to change beyond a new level of enlightenment and the thrill of learning something new.

"Do you know...I feared there might be something wrong with me," she whispered. "For me not to enjoy it."

Helene reached across the table to brace a hand on Clare's shoulder, giving her a look heavy with innuendo. "My dear CeCe, if a woman doesn't enjoy it, there's nothing wrong with her...the fault lies entirely with her lover."

Clare grinned. "So you are saying this is entirely Barnaby's fault?"

"Yes," Helene agreed. "It was entirely Barnaby's fault. Give Edward a chance. Give yourself a chance. I think you'll be pleasantly surprised. As well, I've already written a sizable bank draft to cover his expenses for the next month. You might at least give him thirty days' worth of chances before deciding to put a stop to it."

She huffed with disbelief, still grappling with this notion of men acting as courtesans. It was certainly convenient, she supposed. And, she'd always been a firm believer in equality between the sexes, even in a world that clearly belonged to men. If someone had thought to cater to women in the same way men were privileged to enjoy, then Clare could find no fault with it.

"Well then," she said, peeling off her gloves and setting them aside.

"If he's already been paid for, there seems to be nothing left for me to do but get your money's worth."

The two exchanged mischievous grins before Helene rounded the table and pulled Clare into an embrace.

"Happy birthday, CeCe."

CHAPTER 4

Edward arrived at the Dunnaby residence the following afternoon to find Helene descending the front steps with a valise held in one hand. A carriage waited on the street for her, and a liveried footman stepped forward to accept her baggage as she came off the bottom step. She smiled at the sight of him, the expression reminding him far too much of her niece's wide grin.

"Edward, so good to see you again," she said pausing before the conveyance and turning to face him. "Thank you for returning after yesterday's disastrous beginning. CeCe and I have had the chance to talk it over and she has come to accept my gift."

Relief swept over him at the same time his blood took up a rapid dash away from his brain and toward his groin. He had returned as Helene requested, but hadn't expected to find Clare receptive to his attentions. It had been his aim to kiss her senseless until every protestation died from her lips. Now, it would seem that was hardly necessary.

Instead of voicing any of this, he circled back to the part of her speech that had caught his attention. "CeCe?"

"My pet name for Clare," Helene said with a fond glance at the open front door. "Her middle name is Cecelia, so it only seemed fitting. Anyway, I am off and will not return for at least a fortnight. I thought it best for the two of you to have the house to yourselves while you...grow better acquainted."

Edward raised his eyebrows, wondering how long it would take for him to stop being surprised by this woman's odd relationship with her niece. "Is that so?"

"Quite so. I'll be content in my quiet little villa in Surrey, while the two of you do as you please without worrying that I'm listening. Do be patient with her, Edward. She's as smart as a whip, but at times she thinks too much for my liking. But you don't look like a man who'd have a hard time driving a woman out of her mind."

Edward shifted under her pointed perusal, noting both amusement and appreciation in the eyes that raked him from head to toe. Clearing his throat, he did his best not to blush. "Of course not. She is in good hands."

She glanced down at the hand hanging at his side and pursed her lips. "Good hands, indeed. Good day, Mr. Norton."

"Good day," he replied as she breezed past him, allowing the waiting footman to hand her into the carriage.

Once the vehicle rolled off down the street, Edward turned back to the house where a servant waited for him in the open doorway.

Taking a deep breath, he made his way inside, steeling himself for what would happen next. One thing he could say about this arrangement: he would never be bored. He'd thought the first day would have been spent seducing a virginal spinster, but instead had found himself experiencing her laughter, then her intoxicating kiss, before feeling the sharp side of her tongue. Not exactly what he'd envisioned, yet no less entertaining. He had a feeling no one ever left the presence of Clare Cecelia Dunnaby thinking that the encounter had been uninteresting.

Edward tried to think up some witty or charming greeting as he was led up the curving staircase, but his imagination failed him. Every time he thought of Clare, he remembered those bright eyes spitting blue fire, her lush mouth curling in disdain as she'd expressed her displeasure. While Helene had assured him that Clare had changed her mind, he didn't feel as confident as he ought that she wouldn't toss him out on his ear.

Don't accept defeat, he chided himself. *Desperate times call for desperate measures. You need the money and the only way to it is by getting inside that razor-tongued spinster.*

That razor-tongued spinster happened to have the loveliest mouth he'd ever seen. He'd like to get inside it, too, almost as badly as he'd like to be bollocks-deep inside her cunny.

But first, he needed to keep from doing or saying anything that might cause her to change her mind yet again. Which meant he must comprise a strategy consisting of seduction and complete annihilation of the senses. The effect he'd had on her with a kiss had only worked for so long, which meant he must also be relentless.

The butler paused before a room one door down from the one he'd occupied the day before, and knocked. Clare's muffled voice came from the other side, and the servant pushed the door open. The butler announced him, and she responded that Edward was to be shown into the room.

Though he could not yet see her, the timbre of her voice struck him bone-deep. It was as sensual as the rest of her, slightly deep, throaty. He could imagine her moaning his name, the voice growing huskier, higher in pitch, echoing from the ceiling.

He shook his head to clear it of the thought before he became too aroused to think clearly.

All in good time, Ed, he told himself as he stepped into the room.

His carnal thoughts dissipated the instant he found himself ensconced in Clare's private drawing room. The chamber was unlike anything he'd ever seen, overtaken by a maddening disorder that made his left eye twitch.

Mahogany shelves lined every wall, most of which overflowed with books. Among the tomes were interspersed maps and charts rolled and tied in bundles, a variety of chests in different sizes, ceramic pots and vials, as well as the occasional decorative bookend or paperweight. There were also stacks of books and sheaves of paper covering every available surface—the two desks sitting perpendicular to each other in one corner of the room, the low table near the hearth surrounded by an assortment of mismatched furniture, on the end tables flanking the sofa.

A coat tree stood amid a sea of discarded clothing, enough for her to dress herself as well as several other women.

The rest of the room was comprised of an assortment of things that seemed out of place, yet somehow a harmonious part of this room. There was a collection of Meissen and Sevres figurines lining the mantle, three pedestals holding white sculptures, and a glass-fronted cabinet displaying an Oriental tea service along with several other pieces in the same style such as jugs and vases. Everywhere he glanced, his eye caught some new thing, until he hardly knew where to look.

The sound of a throat clearing solved the dilemma for him, drawing his attention to the woman he'd come to visit. She'd been sitting in one of the armchairs near the hearth, and had left a book face down on the seat when she came to the center of the room to face him.

She wore white today, a color that served to enhance the darkness of her hair and the brightness of her eyes. Those soft, ebony locks teased playfully along her jaw in whimsical waves that made him want to twine his fingers through them and kiss her again. The woman proved as formidable now as she had the day before—back erect, chin raised, eyes boring into him as if analyzing his every trait.

The beginnings of a smile tickled the corner of his mouth as he noticed she wore a pair of spectacles today, the round frames perched on the bridge of her pert nose. They did nothing to hide the things he'd noticed. On the contrary, they enhanced the attributes that made her so damned riveting. The smile almost turned into a wicked grin as he imagined her lying beneath him, wearing nothing but those spectacles.

"Good afternoon," he managed before the silence grew too uncomfortable.

"Thank you for coming," she replied. "And I apologize if I was rude yesterday. I was caught off guard by my aunt's little surprise."

He attempted a step in her direction, then another once he realized she wouldn't retreat. "I hope you weren't too hard on her. She meant well."

A little huff of laughter escaped her, tickling his cheek and sending another jolt of need straight between his legs. Christ, this woman was making a mess of his senses with very little effort.

"That's what she said. Once she explained her reasoning, I could no longer hold a grudge."

That stoked his curiosity, so instead of drawing her against him to pick up where they'd left off, he decided to probe a little deeper.

"Do you mind if I ask what those reasons were? There was not much by way of an explanation, you see. I was simply told that I was being hired for you as a birthday gift. Nothing more."

Clare rolled her eyes and paced away from him a bit, fiddling with one of several glass figurines shaped like flowers lining the edge of one desk.

"I suppose you ought to know, so you can understand my reluctance to enter into such an arrangement. First, I assume you've realized by now that Aunt Helene and I have a most unusual relationship."

"Really?" he teased. "And here I thought it was standard practice for an aunt to purchase a courtesan for her niece."

Those sumptuous lips of hers curved with a grin that made him want to stroke his tongue at the corner of her mouth. "Would that other nieces could be so fortunate. She has always been a bit eccentric, and as the woman who raised me, I suppose she passed the trait along. One of the best things about her, though, is her complete honesty and frankness with me on a variety of subjects. There was never a question I could ask that she wouldn't answer, which has led to a relationship in which we talk about absolutely everything."

Helene's blunt manner of speech and disinterest in propriety had become evident the moment Edward had met her, and aligned with Clare's assessment with her perfectly.

"A rare woman, your aunt," he said. "I take it 'everything' includes the secrets of the bedchamber that are typically kept from young, well-bred ladies."

She chuckled, shaking her head in amused disbelief. "Nothing is a secret with Aunt Helene. She never wanted me to be ignorant about anything, and did not hold back when explaining to me how things work. Well, being the inquisitive person I am, I set out to discover for myself what it was all about."

Edward shouldn't have been surprised. He'd known many bold women in his life, and had even bedded a few. Most were widows, or lightskirts, not virginal chits one might expect to find in a ballroom. To know that she'd gone about taking the rest of her sexual education in hand herself left him both stunned and impressed.

"I see," he replied, for lack of anything better to say. "And the experience was…"

"Unremarkable," she filled in, wrinkling her nose in distaste. "The man I chose was a friend. Not too handsome, but not off-putting either … intelligent, and nice enough. I expected far more than I got from the encounter, and left it thinking that none of it had been worth it. Aunt Helene insisted it would not always be that way, but I had no desire to try again in order to find out. I have far too many interests holding my attention at any given time to worry over such trivial matters."

These last words she said while gesturing about her study, indicating the books and the items he realized she must have taken the time to collect. He supposed it made sense that a woman so interested in intellectual pursuits would have no time to waste on carnal ones, especially given that her first experience had been unexceptional.

"But," she said, with a fluid shrug of one shoulder. "She has convinced me that the problem was a matter of compatibility. According to her, I simply must try again with the right man, and she seems to believe that man is you. So…here I am, ready to give it another go."

Edward was inclined to agree with Helene after their stimulating kiss. Joining Clare at the desk, he reached out to touch her, trailing his fingers from the sleeve of her gown, down the bare skin of her arm. She sucked in a sharp breath, her gaze darting up to meet his as goose-flesh rose up to abrade his fingertips.

"This man...your first lover. Did you feel a strong attraction toward him?"

Her mouth fell open, but words were not immediately forthcoming. She blinked a few times, shivering as he traced slow circles along the inside of her wrist and waited for her answer.

"W-well, he wasn't completely bad to look at—"

"And those porcelain figurines on your mantle are very beautiful," he murmured, leaning in until that scent of lavender invaded his senses in a heady rush. "But I am not *attracted* to them. There's a difference between admiring something in a shop window and wanting it to the point of being ready to empty your purse. Now, this man...did you *want* him, or was he simply a convenient means by which you could discover what making love was like?"

She seemed ready to offer a response, but then halted, snapping her mouth closed with a thoughtful frown. "You know, I've never thought of that way. I liked him well enough. I met him at a botany lecture being held in the home of a friend, and we struck up a rapport. I liked that he was as interested in the study of plants as I was. Mostly, I liked that he was not put off by a woman with thoughts and opinions of her own. But, I do not think I felt any sort of passion toward him. I simply knew he had an interest in me in a physical sense, and that he would be discreet."

He shook his head, running his hand back up toward her neck, then taking a lock of her hair in his grasp. She stiffened, but made no attempt to move away, simply staring at him as he twirled the silken strands around his first finger.

"While I admire your initiative, I must say you went about it all wrong," he declared. "Desire and compatibility are like any other science, you know. The correct variables must be achieved to assure the proper outcome. Surely a learned woman such as yourself must know this."

Her eyes darkened as her pupils grew, turning the sapphire hue to deep indigo. She seemed beyond words now, a tremor going through her as she moved her head in a stiff nod.

"And you should know, your former lover and I have something in common. I, too, find a scholarly mind most stimulating. In fact, I think science to be a downright erotic past time. Shall I demonstrate?"

Before she could respond, he'd taken hold of her shoulders and turned her so that her back was to him. Smoothing both hands down her arms, he lowered his head and nuzzled the side of her neck, enjoying the way it made her shiver against him.

"We must determine the symptoms of a woman who is attracted to the man who wishes to take her to bed," he whispered against the shell of her ear. "First, a quickening of the pulse."

Edward pressed his mouth against the vital vein in her throat, finding to his delight that her pulse fairly galloped against his lips. He nibbled the delectable column of her neck for a moment before humming his satisfaction against her skin.

"Then, there are the tremors," he added. "They begin as very slight vibrations, before turning to full-fledged shivers that can overwhelm the entire body."

She gasped when he kissed the back of her neck, flicking his tongue against the sensitive flesh just beneath her hairline. She shook as he wrapped an arm around her waist, drawing her as tight against him as possible.

"There are other signs of course, ones I can only determine if you'll allow me to properly examine you."

Her head fell against his shoulder, and she went completely pliant in his hold. His cock began a painful and rhythmic throb against the swell of her arse as he caressed his way down her chest—over her collarbone and down to the neckline of her gown. He spotted the lacy edge of a chemise as he dipped his hand inside, biting back a groan at the feel of a pert breast filling his grasp. She whimpered, arching her back and rasping the plump bud of her nipple against his palm. The nub furled tight when he gave her a squeeze, then hardened further when he tugged it gently between his thumb and forefinger.

"Taut nipples," he rasped in her ear, steadily plying the tip of her breast until she began to pant. "Another sure sign."

Continuing to play with the nipple at his fingertips, he slid his other hand down the side of her body and took hold of her skirts. She squirmed against him, agitating the erection rapidly swelling to full mast in his breeches. Slowly drawing her gown up, he found his way toward a stocking-clad leg and tracked a slow path upward. His mouth watered at the first tickle of downy curls against his fingers—curls he knew would be as black as the strands of hair tickling his jaw.

"Wet." He sighed, dipping a finger between her lower lips to find her slick with want. "So, so wet."

One of her hands fell against his thigh, her nails digging in as she seemed to fight for control. She was unraveling, going from cool and reserved to burning hot and he'd hardly touched her yet. Her first lover had been too dense to realize what had been right in front of him. This woman was made for passion; for wild, unbridled ecstasy that only needed the slightest stoking to rise to the surface. That she hadn't enjoyed herself had been entirely his fault, not hers.

It took every ounce of his will to let her skirts fall and pull his hand free of her bodice before turning her to face him. He wanted to tear her clothes off and bend her over the nearest surface before sinking as deep into her as he could go, but he'd done all this to make a point, something he couldn't lose sight of just yet.

Her eyes shined with an unfocused light, as if she were dizzy. Cupping her jaw, he brushed his thumb over her pouting lips, the scent of her arousal filling the air and striking him with a sudden desire to know how she would taste.

"I would say that based upon the exhibited symptoms, you are most certainly attracted to me, Clare," he said, taking hold of her hand and pressing it flat against his chest. "And in case you wish to do your own examination...feel this. My heart is pounding, my pulse is racing..."

She swallowed, glancing to where he held her hand against his heart. "So it is."

"And this."

She let out a strangled sound of shock when he took that same hand and held it against the organ pressing desperately at the fall of his breeches. He resisted the urge to thrust against her hand and simply allowed her to feel the heat and hardness of him, certain that if she concentrated hard enough she might detect the pulse of blood making him feel as if he'd explode at any moment.

"I've been walking around like this since our kiss yesterday, and it shows no signs of going away until I'm inside you," he said, holding her gaze as she closed her fingers over him, seeming more curious than anxious now—as if wanting to know more about the sort of pleasure the hard ridge of flesh could give her. "And now that we have the proper variables in place—you, me, and a rather potent attraction—we must test our hypothesis."

She smiled, and it nearly knocked the air from his lungs with its vivacity. "If Clare engages in intercourse with a man she feels strong desire toward, then she is likely to find the experience more than satis-factory."

Taking her into his arms, he began carrying her toward the sofa facing the hearth.

"Conclusion to be determined," he murmured before taking her mouth in a deep kiss.

CHAPTER 5

Clare felt as if she'd just fallen into some sort of dream as Edward carried her to the sofa without breaking their heated kiss. This *must* be a dream if she could be in the arms of a man feeling as if she would die if he didn't take her then and there. She had *never* experienced such desperate need before, and had never thought she would. The sensations were all completely foreign to her—the tension winding tight as a spring deep within her, the dizziness making her feel as if she couldn't stand on her own two feet, the slow cadence of desire taking up an incessant throb in her cunt. But, rather than run from those feelings as she had during their first kiss, she leaned into them, reveled in them, allowed them to carry her away like the sweeping current of a river.

After all, Edward had appealed to her in a way no one ever had. He hadn't tried to tell her how she ought to feel or what she should want. Instead, he'd shown her all the reasons she ought to give in and enjoy this, all the reasons it would prove to be everything her aunt had promised. And he'd done it with talk of science. He'd used words like hypothesis, variable, and scholarly, whispering them in her ear like the most sensual words ever created.

It had worked like a charm, and now she was clinging to him with her arms and legs as he lowered them to the sofa, arranging her so that she straddled his thighs. Taking hold of the neckline of her bodice, he jerked it down and let her pull her arms free of the sleeves, leaving the garment bunched around her waist. Their fingers met and intertwined at the laces of her stays, but her hands shook too badly to manage it so she allowed him to take over. He worked with swift, deft movements to unlace her and toss the undergarment aside.

Then, bracing his hands against her back, he lunged and fit his mouth against one breast. She gasped and let her head fall back, closing her eyes as he sucked her through the fabric of her chemise. The bud hardened against his tongue, and each suckling pull of his mouth strengthened the pulsations between her legs.

He jerked down the chemise before kissing his way to the other breast. The stroke of his tongue sent a keening cry flying from her lips in startled shock. It was amazing what a difference the absence of a bit of fabric could make. The pleasure seemed magnified with no barriers between them, the rough, hot rasp of his tongue making her feel as if she'd splinter into a thousand pieces.

She writhed in his lap, creating the most delicious friction between them. The fit of his cock against her mons struck her as being stunningly perfect, each movement making her burn hotter and hotter. They worked together to free her from the chemise, a feat that took longer than it should have with Edward refusing to take his mouth off her breast and her inability to sit still. Finally, it fell free of her arms to bare her from the waist up, her clothing falling around her hips like the petals of a white Madonna lily.

He gripped her hips and held her tighter against him, increasing the pressure that made bright spots of light explode within her field of vision. His lips traveled upward from her breasts, leaving hot, open-mouthed kisses along her chest and neck, his tongue flicking at the line of her jaw.

His heavy breaths fanned against the damp spots left by his lips and tongue, each one like a caress all their own. He moved against her, his rhythm a perfect counterpoint to the artless undulations of her hips. The pressure building within her seemed to reach its zenith, culminating with such force that it stole the air from her lungs. Her lips parted on a breathless cry, and she held on to his shoulders, her back arching and her thighs shuddering as exhilarating waves of euphoria rippled through her.

Edward rested his head against her breast and held her tight, slowing the motions of his hips as the little storm within her reached its peak, then abated with gentle tremors that shook her from head to toe.

Falling limp against him, she closed her eyes and drew in deep breaths. She let out a huff of disbelief, unable to believe the speed and intensity of what had just happened.

"Did I just..."

"Spend," Edward murmured between lazy flicks of his tongue against her nipple. "Yes, you did. Most gloriously, I might add."

Sitting up straight, she glanced down to find him watching her with some amusement, and quite a bit of unquenched desire.

"I can't believe that happened when you...you weren't even inside me yet."

The boyish grin that crossed his face affected her almost as much as his use of the word 'variable'. "There's far more to this than me being inside you. For instance..."

She held her breath as he began delving beneath her skirts, his hands stroking up her legs and over the edges of her stockings. The tickle of his fingers against the inside of one thigh made her shiver, the brush of them against her curls turning it into a shudder. She bit her lip and groaned when his touch found her hidden flesh, gliding over the wet folds until he found the throbbing bud of her clitoris. He stroked it with slow, gentle circles—which proved almost more than she could bear after her recent climax.

He began kissing her again, nibbling his way from her neck to her lips. She remained all too aware of the rigid organ pressing against the inside of her thigh, the urgency of it a reminder of what would come next. Where she'd once been uninterested in anything having to do with a man's cock, she now found herself desperate for Edward's.

"When I get you undressed and in a bed, I'll spread you out and have a proper taste," he murmured, slipping one finger into her channel and using his thumb to pick up the slow circling motions. "Then you'll know what it's like to come against my tongue."

She moaned, moving against his hand in a silent plea for more. The invasion of that one finger felt like too much, yet not enough at the same time. Without breaking his stride, he used his free hand to take hold of one of hers.

"Give me a hand, CeCe," he rasped, guiding her into the folds of her gown and petticoats and pressing her palm against his fall.

She fumbled at his buttons, her fingers colliding with his periodically as his finger and thumb went on stroking her to the point of madness. Frustration and desire tangled within her until she could hardly tell one from the other as she did her best to free him without the benefit of sight. That she couldn't see what either of them were doing seemed to heighten the experience, enhancing the feel of him touching her and the heat and hardness of the organ that fell into her palm. She didn't need to see his cock to remember the sight of it from yesterday, hard and jutting out from his body in an impressive display. He let his head fall against the back of the couch and growled, thrusting into her palm as she explored him, her fingers gliding up his shaft and her thumb stroking over the broad head. Wetness smeared her fingers, drawn from him as easily as his touch drew moisture from deep within her.

She emitted an annoyed sigh when his fingers fell away from her, but he only smiled while moving her hand away to take over with his cock. Her disappointment melted into anticipation as he fit the tip against her opening, pushing slowly into her.

Her breath caught in her throat as he began to enter her, his thick cock stretching her with a sharp sting. The discomfort was nothing like she'd experienced her first time, her wetness slicking the way until he'd given her half his length. He took hold of her hips and lifted her before propelling her back down while simultaneously thrusting upward. He filled her to the hilt, pressing his mouth to hers and muffling her startled cry. Her stiffened body went pliant as her channel eased around him, the pulsations taking up a slow rhythm within her once more.

She gave in to the urge to move, taking up the same rhythm she had when pressed against him. Only this time, the pleasure of it was far greater than before, sending deep twinges of ecstasy rippling through her entire being.

"Oh," she whispered, eyes going wide as she met Edwards gaze. "Oh, my God."

He urged her to keep moving, his jaw tight as he met each of her downward motions with thrusts of his hips.

"Don't stop," he ground out. "Take your pleasure, Clare."

His words freed her and she let go, closing her eyes and giving herself over to every wanton urge coming to mind. She threaded her fingers in his hair and kissed him, testing different motions until she found the one that pushed her back toward that elusive precipice. Rocking against him in a slow rhythm, she moaned with each deep plunge of his cock. He kissed every available inch of skin his mouth landed on, his grip on her buttocks tightening as he helped guide her motions, moving with her in a pace so perfect it almost felt as if they'd done this before. Or, as if they were too perfectly matched not to do it right.

This was what she'd been missing. This was what she might never have known if she hadn't opened herself to the possibility. Now that she knew it could be this way, she never wanted it to end.

"You're...wearing...too many clothes," she panted, tangling her fingers in the folds of his cravat.

Edward let out a sound that was half-laugh, half-moan as she began loosening the knot. "You're welcome to remedy that if you wish."

She did wish it. She wanted those supple stretches of skin and muscle bared to her view, hot and solid at her fingertips. Tearing at his buttons with clumsy motions, she allowed him to take control, his hips bucking as he stroked her toward her finish. Pulling his waistcoat and shirt open, she planted her hands on his chest, the wiry, golden hairs tickling her palms. His muscles flexed and heaved with every motion, the hypnotic sight captivating her to the point of distraction. She explored him with her touch, then lowered her head to kiss him as he'd done her, lingering in the places that produced sounds of pleasure from deep in his throat. She wanted more of him—wanted them both undressed with every naked inch pressed together—but there was no time. Climax loomed near and she forgot everything other than chasing it to its conclusion. Gripping his shoulders, she met his swift strokes with her own desperate movements, grinding against him with wild abandon.

He cupped her breast, and a light pinch of her nipple sent her over the edge. Her sheath clenched around him, powerful spasms shaking her to her core as the world around her faded until nothing existed except for him inside of her. She fell atop him with a rough exhale, becoming formless and weightless in his arms. His harsh breaths against her neck and the shudders wracking him told Clare he would soon follow. But, she could only cling to him as he pounded into her a few more times before pulling free with a ragged moan, spending into the obscurity of her skirts.

The tension melted from his body, and he kept one arm around her while sinking into the sofa cushions, his harsh breaths mingling with her own swift pants. She nuzzled into the warm haven of his chest, noticing for the first time that he smelled of oakmoss and cedar. Inhaling the woodsy scent, she closed her eyes and rested in the moment. Unlike the end of her short and unsatisfying tryst with Baldwin Barnaby, Clare found she was content to linger with Edward, enjoying the pleasant twinge between her legs that reminded her so poignantly of what they'd just done.

Already, she wanted more, every bit of what the next thirty days would bring. A smile stretched her lips as she realized a month might never be enough. Edward would never find himself without a keeper if he treated her to such ecstasy every time he took her to bed.

Shifting beneath her, he lifted her chin until she met his gaze. That darling smile of his was back, making her want to kiss him before tumbling them both to the floor and begging him for more.

"Conclusion?" he asked, his grin turning wicked.

Returning his smile, she propped her chin in her hand. "The

hypothesis has been proven correct...for now. I do believe we ought to conduct further tests to ensure we were truly correct."

He reached up to adjust her spectacles, which had been knocked askew during their frenzied coupling. "I am happy to continue acting as a most willing test subject."

CHAPTER 6

Edward gazed at the woman sprawled atop him, her nude upper body bared to his gaze, the sheets tangling with her long legs. After gathering the strength to leave the couch, they had finished undressing, leaving their clothing in a heap on the floor of her study before adjourning to Clare's bedroom. There, surrounded by opulent decor, they'd fallen into bed together. He found himself startled to realize that he wanted her again only minutes after having been inside her, the acute sensation of arousal overwhelming him the moment he'd gotten her naked body in his arms. But, while he realized this hadn't been her first time, she'd been as tight as a virgin when he'd first penetrated her. He supposed it had been some time since her first abysmal lover, and that meant he ought not attempt to take her again so soon. Which meant going no further than the occasional kiss, though his hands did wander now and then. How could they not with such a tempting creature in his arms?

She was even more alluring in the aftermath of their fucking, her hair a wavy mess around her face, her eyes bright and shining, her spectacles set aside on the washstand. It surprised him to notice that she hadn't retreated from him afterward, something he'd expected at the onset. But it seemed that once a person managed to get Clare to open up, she remained that way, her smiles wide and her eyes hiding nothing. He hadn't needed her to say it aloud for him to know she had enjoyed herself, but it had certainly been nice to have confirmation. Now, not only was he secure in the knowledge that he wouldn't have to worry about money for the next month, he had finally assuaged his curiosity over what it would be like to bed her.

"I don't understand it," he murmured, reaching out to tuck a lock of her hair behind one ear.

"Don't understand what?" she asked, propping her chin on his chest and gazing up at him.

"How no one has discovered the little spitfire I was just introduced to. I came here intending to seduce you, then fuck you into a mindless stupor. What I didn't expect was for *you* to fuck *me* within an inch of my life."

She threw her head back and laughed, that unrestrained, boisterous sound he couldn't hear enough of. It brightened the room, filling it with light and sound.

"I suppose it's because I never allowed anyone to uncover that part of me. Really, I had no idea it existed. After that first time I saw no need to repeat the experience. I had a number of other interests to devote my time and passion to."

"So I noticed," he remarked, inclining his head in the direction of her study. "Your interests have quite overtaken that room. It's a wonder you don't get lost in there."

This time she released a soft, girlish giggle. It made him want to make her laugh again so he could go on listening to that musical sound for what remained of the day.

"If I do not make an appearance by lunchtime, Aunt Helene often braves the study to ensure I haven't been swallowed by the clutter. No one else seems to understand it, but while it all looks very disordered I know where everything is. If I allow the servants to clean, I'll never be able to find a thing."

Thinking back to the collections filling the next room, he asked the one question that had been on his mind from the moment he'd stepped inside.

"What sorts of things do you collect? I gathered that is the purpose of the chests and shelves?"

She nodded, her chin digging into his chest. He adjusted her so her head rested on the pillow beside his.

"Quite a number of things," she replied. "It began with watches when I was a girl. I've always been fascinated with them, and the number of designs that exist. In that room there is a chest containing forty-seven watches."

He smirked at her. "Only forty-seven?"

"I happen to be *very* particular about watches," she said with a haughty sniff. "I seek out only the most unique designs, and have an affinity for gaudy, overblown styles. Then, there's my collection of geological specimens."

"Rocks?" he asked with a little smirk. "I used to collect those when I was a boy—pebbles and stones. None of them were very remarkable now that I think of it, but you couldn't have convinced me of that back then."

"Minerals," she corrected, her voice taking on that governess-like quality which made his cock react in the most intriguing way. "The sorts that, when broken open, reveal the most stunning crystallized formations on the inside. A friend of mine is a geologist, and during her travels she excavates and sends me samples of her discoveries for my collection."

"Don't you ever accompany her on these excavations?"

"Occasionally, though recently her travels have taken her farther from home for longer periods of time. I do not like to leave Aunt Helene for so long, so I've settled for living vicariously through Gilly and her letters."

"Your aunt doesn't strike me as needing a companion or caretaker," he said, remembering the sight of the spry woman rushing down the front steps to get off to her villa. The woman appeared to possess the vitality of one half her age.

"No," Clare agreed. "But I owe her everything. She took us in—my sister, Alice, and I—after we lost both our parents to scarlet fever. She'd been recently widowed, but brought us into her home without hesitation and gave us the best years of her life, raising us as if we were her own. Alice left us to wed a few years ago and never looked back. I believe she thinks herself above us, her being the wife of a baron now and the two of us a scandalous widow and a bluestocking spinster."

Edward didn't have to meet this Alice woman to decide he did not like her. The hurt in Clare's voice told him all that he needed to know. Her sister's abandonment had dealt quite a blow to herself as well as Helene.

"I'd choose the widow and the bluestocking over the baron any day," he said, trying to inject a bit of lightness into his tone.

It worked, producing another one of her smiles, and she rolled onto her back, hands folded over her abdomen. "We've both come to accept that Alice has her life apart from us. Aunt Helene takes comfort in my presence, so I am happy to remain here with her."

But what of marriage and a family of your own?

The question nearly fell off the tip of his tongue, but he clamped his lips around it. He hardly knew this woman, despite their recent intimacy. They were getting on so well, he did not want to ruin it with such talk. As beautiful and vivacious as she was, Edward could imagine that Clare had had a challenging time finding her match. A woman with her blunt tongue, independent streak, and love of science would intimidate a man without the bollocks to accept her being smarter than him. And those who did take an interest in her keen mind seemed lacking in other regards, like her first lover. It was no wonder she spent so much of her time with watches and rocks.

"What else have you got stashed in that room?" he prodded, turning the conversation onto a safer path.

"Porcelain figurines—Dresden and Sevres specifically. More porcelain from the Orient, tea services and vases and such. Oh, and this doesn't qualify as a collection, but there is a small conservatory built off the back of the house. It takes up most of the courtyard in place of a garden—another one of Aunt Helene's extravagant birthday gifts."

Edward propped himself up on his elbow and gazed down at her, his interest piqued by the mention of her birthday. "You alluded to your aunt's birthday gifts before. I assume she always makes such a big production of celebrating it."

Clare snorted. "Always. When Alice and I were girls, she began the tradition of treating our birthdays as some sort of grand holiday. Looking back, I do believe she was doing her best to ensure we did not miss our parents so much on those days. Such times were difficult in the beginning—birthdays, Christmas, New Year's Eve. Even though it was hardly necessary as we grew older, she persisted. Each year she tries to outdo herself."

"And what of this year?" he teased, gently tugging a lock of her dark hair. "Has this year's gift outshone that of your last birthday?"

With a giggle, she turned to face him, snaking a hand around his waist and molding her soft body against his. The arousal he'd been trying to ignore for the past hour became even more urgent.

"Most certainly," she murmured, winding her hips in a wicked motion that had him pressing even closer. "After all, that hot air balloon ascension lasted a mere hour."

"Never let it be said that I cannot outlast a hot air balloon," he murmured against her mouth just before engaging her in a kiss.

She opened to him readily now, hooking one leg over his hip and arching against him in invitation. He palmed her arse and ground against her, enjoying her soft whimpers against his lips at the brush of his cock against her tender, wet inner flesh.

He entered her with ease, groaning into her mouth at the tight, hot clench of her cunny around him. After their first frenzied encounter, he was content to take his time now, gliding in and out of her with slow, languid strokes. He drew it out for as long as he could, eventually rolling her onto her back, then arranging her on her hands and knees, ensuring she knew without question that there was so much more to making love than her first bedmate had shown her. He held back his own climax for as long as he could, bringing her to completion three times and ensuring he put in a more spectacular performance than a bloody hot air balloon. Pulling away from her at the last possible second, he spilled on the sheets, then gathered her into his arms again as she began drifting off to sleep.

As he lay there sinking into slumber himself, it occurred to Edward that if he weren't careful, he might find himself in a precarious situation. After all, what man could hold a living, breathing flame in his arms and not become consumed? If he allowed it, he could become obsessed with a woman like Clare Cecelia Dunnaby.

"MAY I ASK YOU A RATHER PERSONAL QUESTION?" CLARE ASKED hours later from across the dining room table.

After they'd awakened, his growling stomach had sent her into a fit of giggles, then prompted her to invite him to stay and dine with her. Since he knew his sister had plans with a friend and her chaperone for the evening, he had no pressing reason to return home. He also had no desire to dine alone, so he had taken her up on her offer.

Retrieving his discarded clothing, he'd put himself together as well as he could manage while she had retreated to her dressing room. Before long they were ensconced in the dining room with several dishes spread out between them and lit tapers casting a warm glow over the intimate setting. She had banished the servants so they could be alone, and they'd been serving themselves from the various offerings filling the table.

They had eaten in companionable silence until now, when Clare's question had broken through the quiet.

"Of course you can," he replied.

After all the things she'd revealed about her family and her first unremarkable experience with intercourse, he certainly didn't feel as if he had the right to hold back. Besides, they were as well acquainted physically as two people could be at this point. What could it hurt to let her know something about him other than the feel of his hands, mouth, and cock?

Pausing with a cluster of peas in her spoon, she glanced up at him, seeming prepared to mince words for the first time since he'd met her. Which could mean only one thing.

"You want to know how I became a courtesan," he stated, taking the burden of finding the right words off her shoulders.

She flushed pink, but gave a swift nod. "I'm simply curious. I never knew male courtesans existed, so I find myself wanting to know how a man comes into such a profession."

Slouching a bit in his chair, he reached for his wineglass. "I actually did not know male courtesans existed either, until very recently. I happen to be friends with a man who's been at it for a year, and he told me it's been quite lucrative for him. I decided it wouldn't be such a hardship, bedding a beautiful woman for money."

For a moment, he wondered if she would find such a sentiment distasteful. Bedding a man who'd been bought with a bank draft was far different than discussing it over dinner.

But, he ought to have expected her to simply peer at him through her spectacles with an inquisitive look and launch into her next question.

"So...I am your first keeper then?"

"You are."

She took a sip of her wine and then smiled at him. "Am I what you expected?"

"No," he replied. "You're better than I expected, in more ways than one."

"I do take pleasure in surprising people."

"Well, you achieved that the moment you burst out laughing after learning why I was naked in your bed. In all my twenty-seven years of life, I've never been more shocked."

"That was not well done of me. I hope you didn't take it as an insult to you as a person, Edward. Truly, I was convinced Aunt Helene was having me on."

He waved away her concern. "That much was clear enough. Besides, I found your laugh to be as enchanting as the rest of you."

"I've been told it's too loud, not ladylike enough. Alice was always warning me that it would scare prospective suitors away. Can you imagine such a thing? A room full of men, intimidated by a laugh of all things."

Edward could actually imagine it. He could see how everything about her might intimidate some men, and that laugh revealed more about her than she likely realized. It said that she cared nothing for the judgment of others, that she was as boisterous and free as that laughter, and that she could not be made to fit the mold of the other London chits. Most of all, it said that she would never be content to live under anyone's rule, be it the dictates of society or a husband's dominance.

"I think it ridiculous to stifle something as natural as a laugh just to keep from drawing attention to oneself. So I laugh as loud and as often as I want."

"Well done," he murmured, raising his glass to her before taking a sip.

They lapsed into silent eating again, but that did not seem to suit Clare, for she soon came up with another question to volley at him.

"The amount my aunt is paying for these thirty days. Will it be enough? I assume there's a pressing need for it."

Thinking over the pile of unpaid bills overrunning the office of Norton & Rivers, he experienced a bitter taste in his mouth. "Honestly, I am not certain. You see, my father recently died and left the family business in my hands."

"Oh, I'm so sorry," she whispered, perusing his austere black attire as if just noticing it for the first time.

"It has been a difficult time for my family—or what's left of it anyway. We lost my mother years ago, so I've been left with the care of my little sister as well as my younger brother, who has recently completed university."

Her brow furrowed with concern, she reached out to lay her hand atop his. "That's a devil of a burden for one man to bear alone."

It was, and damn if he wasn't already exhausted from holding it up. Between Caroline and her complaints over their diminished fortunes, and Jacob's obliviousness to it all, he'd begun to feel as if he weren't up to the task to taking over the family business as well. Even with his pockets filled for the time being, it all seemed so insurmountable.

Edward found it easy to confide in her due to the comfort they'd seemed to fall into, so he shared his thoughts without reservation.

"It might not be so bad if not for the fact that the business is failing. My father was a good man—a wonderful father, and a kind person—but he was abominable when it came to managing money. What I thought I knew about the state of the family finances turned out to be only a fraction of the truth. So, I am now the proud owner of a shipping company without warehouses to store goods in, ships that are incapable of carrying cargo, or a partner. There is also a mountain of debt, which has ruined the reputation of the line. In short, none of it could be mended without money—which I had very little of until your aunt hired me for you."

Clare did not respond at first, folding her hands atop the table and staring at him with a pensive expression. When she finally spoke, her voice held not a trace of humor or artifice.

"I think what you've done is very admirable."

He blinked, momentarily taken aback by that praise. "It is?"

This time, her smile was soft and small but no less genuine as she met and held his gaze. "Of course it is. You've been faced with a difficult situation, and rather than lament the cruelty of fate or allow everything to fall apart around you, you've found a way to turn things around. Quite an inventive way, and one that takes advantage of your talents."

He grinned. "By talents, do you mean seducing scholarly women with the use of scientific terms?"

Her gaze grew heated, the brilliant irises darkening a shade. "Among other things."

Laying his fork beside his empty plate, he shrugged. "I suppose it is easy to think of what I'm doing as some sort of noble effort for the sake of my family when you have been my one and only keeper thus far."

She shook her head in disagreement. "If a hundred women had come before me, my opinion would remain unchanged. Though, I cannot say I might not suffer a bit of envy."

"Do not worry, CeCe. You're the only woman I've ever seduced with talk of science."

Raising her glass, she beamed at him in a way that made him feel ten feet tall. "To making the best of things, even when they're at their worst."

Lifting his glass, he clinked it against hers. "To being taken by surprise."

CHAPTER 7

Clare sat across the small, rough wooden table from Edward, watching as he dug into the bowl before him with enthusiasm. A few days following their first night together, he had suggested they have their dinner at one of his favorite haunts. According to Edward, the intimate coffee house nestled in Covent Garden had the best Indian cuisine to be found in London. Downstairs, the men enjoyed their tea, coffee, or curries. Meanwhile, Edward had requested the use of a private room, sneaking her in through a back entrance to avoid Clare being noticed. He'd wanted her to enjoy the food without having to worry over the ruin that would be made of her reputation by setting foot in a male haunt.

While traveling Europe with Aunt Helene, Clare had tasted a variety of new foods. But, she'd never sampled the robust, spicy fare laid out before them in various dishes and platters.

"Try the curry," Edward urged between bites. "I wager you've never tasted anything so good."

Glancing down at the heavily sauced chicken and mound of steaming rice before her, she lifted her spoon. Edward watched her with parted lips, as if anticipating her taking the first bite. She obliged him, scooping a portion of the chicken, the aromatic spices wafted up her nostrils. Her eyes widened at the abundance of flavors exploding across her tongue, accentuated by a burst of heat that she found both pleasant and tear-inducing. Blinking her watering eyes, she met Edward's gaze.

"Oh my," she murmured, taking a spoonful of the rice, then reaching out for a disk of the flat bread resting between them. Edward had referred to it as *naan*.

"Do you like it?" he asked with a smile.

"Very much," she murmured, following his lead and taking both the rice and the curry onto her spoon to combine them. "I must send for some to be delivered at home so Aunt Helene can try it."

"The two of you are sure to become as enamored with the food as I am. An old school friend of mine would invite me home with him between terms, and his cook was from Calcutta. I leaped at the chance to join him every chance I got, even though I knew I'd fall prey to the matchmaking schemes of his mother. She had three young daughters, two of whom were nearing marriageable age."

She giggled at the face he made, as if his curry had suddenly turned sour. "I take it that like most bachelors you've spent years avoiding the matrimonial noose."

He paused for a moment, fiddling with his spoon. "Perhaps not avoiding it in the way you might think. I'm not opposed to marriage, and if the right woman were to come along at the right time, I'd be happy to settle down and begin a family of my own."

She supposed that shouldn't come as much of a surprise. The more she came to learn about Edward, the clearer it was that family meant a great deal to him. Caring for his siblings was what had driven him to become her courtesan.

Curiosity urged her to press further.

"Has there ever been anyone...a woman you considered for marriage?"

He tore his gaze from hers, staring down into his bowl. "I haven't let myself consider it. Not now, when my life is a shambles. I have nothing to offer a wife and my family name is now synonymous with shoddy business practices."

The dejection in his voice pricked her somewhere deep within her chest. It wasn't pity, exactly. It was more of a deep sorrow she felt knowing that his family's financial woes had hindered him from opening himself to the possibility of love and marriage.

"Any woman who can't look past your family name or temporary circumstances isn't worth marrying," she declared, her voice grown heavy and thick with emotion.

Edward wasn't like her, she could see that clearly. She had closed herself off to the idea of a husband and children, had made up her mind that it simply wasn't as important as she'd first believed. But his words had been revealing, and now she could all but see the need radiating from him in visible currents. The need to have something of his own that hadn't been handed down by his father—something that wasn't a failing business, or a mountain of debt, or two siblings who needed his care.

Reaching across the table with his free hand, he intertwined his fingers with hers. "I am flattered you think so. But I cannot blame any woman for wanting a secure future. Once I am able to provide that, I suppose I can then turn my mind to marriage."

"Whoever your bride happens to be, she'll be fortunate to have you."

The moment the words fell from her lips, Clare's mind overwhelmed her with thoughts of Edward with another woman. Kissing her. Holding her. Making love to her without pulling away at the end with the hopes that it would result in a child. Clearing her throat, she pulled her hand from his grasp. It was ridiculous of her to feel a bit of jealousy over a nonexistent woman, especially when their association was based on nothing more than carnal desires and a bank draft.

"What of you?" Edward asked.

Pausing after a sip of tea, she frowned. "What about me?"

"You made it clear that you had no interest in intimate relations. Does that indifference apply to marriage as well?"

"I'm not really indifferent," she replied. "Merely resigned to the fact that what I want might not really exist."

She glanced up to find him watching her, his stare pensive and probing.

"And what do you want?"

Clare mulled that over for a moment before answering. It wasn't that she didn't know what she wanted—she'd always known. She simply did not know how to express it out loud in a way that wouldn't make her sound completely insane. Still, she gave it a most valiant effort.

"Well, I am not keen on the idea of being married just for the sake of it. It does not bother me one bit to be called a spinster or to be viewed as somehow less than my peers for failing to secure a match. If I ever marry—a prospect that becomes less likely with each passing year—it will be because I've met the man I simply cannot live without. It does not seem worth it to me otherwise. But, as I said...I am not certain such a phenomenon truly exists. Love seems like such an abstract notion to me. Elsewise, why would it be so elusive?"

She looked away then, certain he would think she was mad. People married for all sorts of reasons that had nothing to do with love. Especially women, who must consider their futures as well as things such as status and money. Men needed heirs to carry on family legacies. Rarely did any of it involve love, and married couples seemed to get on just fine without it.

However, she was surprised to glance up and find Edward's gaze still locked on her, the intensity of it deepened as he brushed his fingers against hers in a feather-light gesture. Her breath caught and held as he did it again, tracing the tip of his finger along the edge of hers, sending shivers racing up her arm.

"I don't think it is as elusive as you think," he murmured, interlacing their fingers and fitting his palm against hers. "Difficult to find, perhaps, but not impossible. And I do not think it's unreasonable for you to want it. You deserve nothing less, CeCe."

Her throat began to burn from how long it took her to remember how to breathe, her insides erupting into a confusing ripple of unnamed emotion. With a little shake of her head, she reminded herself that Edward was a courtesan. It was his job to seduce her in bed as well as out of it. Perhaps he truly did believe in love, and maybe he thought her a good person worthy of the sort of marriage she would want if the opportunity presented itself. That wasn't a good enough reason for her heart to pound, her palms to grow damp, and her chest to swell with hope.

"Thank you," she said, her voice low and strained.

Pulling her hand away, she gave him a small smile. His intense expression melted away and his boyish grin appeared, putting her at ease. She'd revealed more to him in a few days than she ever had to another living soul. Perhaps it was nothing more than a side-effect of the sort of intimacy she'd always avoided. She supposed it was nice to have someone to confide in along with the other obvious pleasures.

As they resumed their meal and the light, easy banter that had begun the night, she told herself that it didn't have to mean anything, except perhaps that she'd gained a friend of sorts as well as a lover. It certainly did not mean that the hope unfurling from some hidden place deep within her had anything to do with him.

When Helene returned to London a fortnight later, she entered the townhouse to find Clare setting an arrangement of fresh-cut blossoms from the greenhouse. Approaching the round table gracing the center of the entrance hall, she watched as Clare worked to get the placement of lilies, roses, and jasmine just right. She'd spent a pleasant morning with her plants, notating the pleasing progress of her hybrids, which had produced bright green sprouts a few days ago. They continued to grow as she kept the soil damp and ensured they received ample light on sunny days. She anticipated they would begin to bud and blossom in a few more weeks, revealing the results of her experiment.

"Welcome home," she said, standing back to study her work. "How was your time away?"

"Quiet, and a nice reprieve from this overcrowded city for a time," her aunt replied, reaching out to caress the petals of a bright red rose. "This is lovely. Such vibrant colors."

Clare peered at her over the tangle of flowers and pursed her lips, certain that the last thing her aunt wanted to talk about right now was a flower arrangement. An entire fortnight had passed since Helene had left her to enjoy her birthday gift in relative privacy. It wouldn't be long before she'd begin prodding Clare for details.

"Shall I send for tea? I'm sure you must be famished after your journey."

Handing her wrap off to a footman, Helene gave Clare a pointed look. "Oh, very well, if it will get us to the matter at hand that much faster. Send for the tea, and cakes while you're at it. Then, you are going to tell me everything."

Clare couldn't hold in a laugh as her aunt sauntered past her into the nearest drawing room, where a fire had just been stoked in anticipation of her arrival. She took her time finishing her arrangement and sending for the tea, finding a perverse sense of satisfaction in making Helene dangle a bit.

When, at last, they sat before the fire with filled teacups and a silver tower of various confections between them, Helene leaned forward and made her demands.

"Out with it," she prodded. "I did not receive any messages from you bemoaning your decision to enjoy my gift. So, I can only assume things have been going well?"

Unable to remain aloof any longer, Clare let her lips split into a wide smile. "Better than well. Edward and I have been getting on famously. You were right about everything. All I needed was to experiment with the right variables."

Her aunt's face transformed into a mask of smugness. "I knew Edward had all the proper...variables. I could tell just by looking at him. I've always been good at that, you know."

Clare did know it. While she'd been widowed for decades, Helene had never wanted for male companionship. She'd always been discreet, but Clare was no fool. There had been a number of affairs over the years, all of which had seemed to make her aunt happy enough. Now, she understood why.

"Tell me more, dear," Helene demanded, setting the tea aside and bracing her chin on one hand like a young girl indulging in juicy gossip.

So, Clare told her everything without delving too deeply into the intimate details. She'd seen Edward almost every evening for the past fortnight and had even spent a few afternoons with him as well. He'd displayed an interest in her work with lilies, so she'd taken him into her conservatory and explained her hybrid experiments to him. She had even guided him through collecting newly cultivated seeds and planting them in their own pots, taking notes on the process in her journal. He'd laid her over an empty space on one of her tables and lifted her skirts afterward, claiming that her use of scientific names and terminology had worked him into quite a state. It had been exhilarating, surrendering to passion while surrounded by the perfume of flowers, the glass ceiling allowing the sun to shine down on them, and the threat of discovery by a passing servant adding a bit of a thrill to it all.

They'd attended the theater one night, and he had escorted her to a dinner party the following evening, which had been nothing more than an excuse for the host to gather with others sharing an interest in botany. Edward had held his own during the affair, listening intently to the discussions on cross-breeding and classification while asking questions without seeming to worry that it showed just how little he knew on the subject. He seemed open to learning about something she loved, which made her like him as more than just a bedmate.

Though, in that regard he proved quite spectacular. After their first few nights together, she had begun to worry that the novelty of it would begin to wear thin. However, he continued to prove her wrong, bringing something new and wonderful to each encounter. She found a freedom in bed with him that she'd never known. He liked her loud laugh, her spectacles, her short hair. He claimed that her bosom wasn't too small no matter what she said and seemed to think the sight of her naked was the most diverting thing he'd ever seen. That made it easy to come to him without reservation, and with an eagerness to learn all she could about passion and desire.

"So," Helene said once Clare had finished filling her in. "Does this mean you want to keep him a bit longer than thirty days? The owner of the agency assures me that the contract can be extended for however long you wish."

Staring down into the murky depths of her teacup, Clare mulled that over. It wasn't the first time the notion had come to mind, and her aunt had just reminded her that she'd yet to make a decision on that front.

"I like him," she confessed. "As more than just a lover. I enjoy the time we spend out of bed as much as in it."

"Then you certainly need more time with him. That sort of compatibility does not happen often, as you well know. Why not enjoy it?"

Clare took a few sips of tea before answering. While on one hand she agreed with her aunt that she ought to enjoy this while it lasted, she also understood that more time could cause her to become hopelessly entangled with Edward. That much had already been proved the night of their conversation over Indian cuisine. He'd delved far too deep into her deepest longings, and now they'd been brought to the surface.

Upon her coming out and first Season she'd grown bored with the men she was supposed to consider for marriage. There had been the men who'd treated her as if she had some sort of contagious disease because she'd rather discuss politics and science than the weather. There had been those who'd displayed interest in her, but they were either as boring as doorknobs or their interest had turned out to be purely carnal in nature. Until now, there had been no need to think of such matters, but now she could not help but wonder how things might end if she allowed this arrangement to last much longer. An unexpected surge of yearning shot through her, shocking Clare with its intensity. For the first time in a long while she longed for more—for companionship and intimacy, and the sorts of things that could only last a short time with a man like Edward.

"He's come into this arrangement expecting it to last for thirty days. If I end it as planned, we both walk away having gained what we originally sought with no harm done. But, what if we carry on another month, or three, or six? How much harder will it become to part ways then?"

Arching an eyebrow, Helene perused her with pensive eyes. "I suppose that all depends. Are you worried it will be harder for Edward, or yourself?"

"Myself, I suppose. He's only doing this in order to save his family's failing business and care for his siblings. One keeper will do as well as another for his purposes, whereas I..."

I will be devastated to become attached to him, only to realize the feeling is not mutual.

"You've never had both a friend and a lover in the same man before. You worry that you'll want more from him than he's willing or able to give."

Dash it all, she didn't want to admit it, but her aunt's words were true. Her pride stung as she was forced to admit that what she feared most was heartbreak. Though they were having the most wonderful time, he did not express tender sentiments or an inkling that he ever desired a more permanent liaison. Edward had the potential to make her want the things she'd convinced herself she could live without. And it would destroy her when it turned out he didn't want to go on giving them to her forever.

Reaching out to touch her hand, Helene drew Clare's gaze, her expression one of determination and understanding. "Only you can decide whether it will be worth it in the end. Sometimes, people are meant to enrich our lives for a short time. The trick is, learning when to let them go. Whatever you decide, I am glad you gave this a chance at all. There are some experiences a woman should never miss, and a good, thorough tupping is one of them."

That little quip got a smile out of her, lifting her mood a bit. Perhaps Aunt Helene was right and she was simply over-thinking the matter. Edward would be a temporary part of her life that she'd enjoy until it was over—like a spicy curry, or warm summer rain, or the short life of a fresh-cut rose.

"Aunt Helene, however did you come to be so wise?"

"Experience and age," her aunt replied with a shrug. "When you get to be as old as I am, wisdom comes along with the gray hairs."

"Oh, rubbish," Clare snorted. "You're no more old than I'm a duck."

"You only say that because I've never told you my real age."

"When *will* you tell me how old you are? I'm twenty-one now."

"And you *still* aren't old enough to know the truth. Ask me again when you turn thirty. The revelation of how ancient I truly am will be my gift to you that year. Now, come. We have just enough time to take a walk before dinner."

Happy for the temporary diversion, Clare left the drawing room with her aunt. They parted ways to fetch hats, gloves, and coats, with Clare deciding that her misgivings concerning Edward could be forgotten for now. Too much worry would hamper the fun of it, and they still had a fortnight left.

EDWARD GLANCED UP FROM THE LEDGERS BEFORE HIM AS THE DOOR to Norton & Rivers swung open. Squinting against the sudden flash of light, he discovered that Hugh and Benedict had come to call. These days, anyone who knew him understood that his mornings and afternoons were mostly spent within the office of the shipping line, where he worked tirelessly to set things right. After the first official day of his and Clare's arrangement, he'd felt secure in delving into the funds Benedict had given him after taking his percentage.

His first order of business had been to pay the debts owed to the suppliers and craftsman, then ordering the goods needed to repair the damaged ships. He'd been told that at least three of them could be prepared to sail within a fortnight, and sure enough he'd received word just yesterday that those repairs had been completed, the vessels ready for cargo and a crew. While waiting, he had thrown himself into gaining back a few of the sailors who had worked for his father, who in turn had recruited as many of their previous mates as possible. He appointed a captain for each ship and had charged them with assembling full crews as soon as possible.

This afternoon, he would secure warehouses for goods, which would complete the groundwork enabling him to court their lost clientele back to the line. It was his hope to have the first ships at sea within the month, which would be enough to provide the first income the business had seen in half a year.

After paying the business' debts, he had increased the wages of the woman acting as both his cook and housekeeper, then given both Caroline and Jacob a small stipend to purchase new clothing. He'd even been able to give them both a bit of pin money for the time being. They'd been thrilled with even so small an amount to spend on themselves, but he had assured them there was more to come. He'd begin searching for new lodgings and hiring on more servants once the first shipments were secured and he was certain the flow of income could become a steady trickle.

"Sorry to interrupt," Hugh said as Benedict closed the door, leaving them with tapers and the open shutters for light. "You must be terribly busy."

"For once, being terribly busy involves making money as opposed to losing it, so I don't mind it much," Edward replied, gesturing toward the set of chairs facing his desk. "Please, sit down."

While they made themselves comfortable, Edward set his pen aside and stoppered his inkwell. Benedict removed his hat and rested it on his knee, casting a curious glance about the empty office. Edward had dusted and polished the furniture, but had done little in the way of sprucing up the space. That seemed trivial when his ships were only just being repaired, but it stood among the things he wished to accomplish in the near future.

"We don't want to take up too much of your time," Benedict said, his gaze coming to rest on Edward once again. "It is customary for me to look in on new courtesans to assure they are settling into their first arrangements well."

He couldn't help the smile that came to his lips as Benedict's words brought Clare to mind. He'd parted ways with her at sunrise this morning, loath to leave her warm bed but needing to return home and freshen up before coming into the office. They had plans to share dinner this evening, which of course would lead them straight back to the bed. Their time together had been brief, but he found himself thinking of her often while working, and looking forward to returning to her when he'd finished for the day.

"Clare and I are getting along just fine," he replied. "She's a lovely woman and quite a joy to be with."

Hugh raised his eyebrows, almost seeming surprised by this news. "Well, that's certainly a bonus. You never know what you are going to get when introduced to a new keeper. All the better if you find you actually like her."

"Has she given any indication that she'd like to extend her contract beyond the agreed-upon thirty days?" Benedict asked. "I'd like to know if I need to begin considering a new keeper for you."

The thought of leaping straight from Clare's bed into another woman's left a bitter taste in his mouth. It wasn't a problem he'd ever had in his past dealings with women, but then most of his previous experience with the fairer sex had never gone beyond the bedchamber. Acting as a courtesan required him to cater to Clare out of bed as well as in it, and he found he actually enjoyed that part of it. There was always some new facet of her personality to unearth, and she never ceased taking him by surprise.

However, as the head of the agency it made sense for Benedict to think of this in terms of pounds and pence. In truth, Edward couldn't afford not to follow the other man's lead. Should Clare decide she was finished with him two weeks from now, he'd need to consider the detriment of going without the additional income a new keeper could offer him. It could take months, or even a year, for him to feel comfortable supporting his family with the line as his only source of capital.

"Not yet," he replied. "We haven't really had time to discuss it."

Really, the subject had never come up. If Clare hadn't expressed interest in continuing on with him, perhaps that was because there was no interest. That proved a clear enough answer to the unspoken question. He didn't want to dwell on why that made his heart sink and his stomach ache.

"Find out, and inform me of the answer," Benedict said. "The sooner we know what to expect, the better."

For lack of anything to say, Edward simply nodded his agreement. How the devil was he to ask Clare such a thing without seeming like an insensitive ass or a desperate beggar? He supposed that was his problem, so he would puzzle it out on his own time.

Retrieving his watch, Benedict flipped it open and frowned. "I'm sorry, but if I don't leave now I'll be late for an appointment. Edward, feel free to call on me if you need anything. I'll be ready to make the proper arrangements when necessary."

"Of course," he said as Benedict rose and donned his hat once more. "And thank you for everything. This arrangement has solved a hell of a problem for my family and I am grateful."

Tipping his hat, Benedict gave him a ghost of a smile. "All in the line of duty. Hugh, will you stay?"

Hugh waved Benedict off, seeming in no hurry to leave his seat. "Yes, you go on. I wouldn't want to hold you up."

A moment later, the door opened and then closed, leaving Edward and Hugh alone. Releasing a sigh, Edward slumped in his chair. He supposed he liked Benedict well enough, but didn't know him as well as he did Hugh. Perhaps his longtime friend could offer him some insight on how to proceed.

"How do you do it?" he murmured, running a hand through his hair.

"Do what?" Hugh asked.

"Pass from one woman to the next without a look back. I thought it would be easy, but I'm finding the notion difficult to swallow. I like Clare quite a lot, and...well, what if the woman who comes after her doesn't measure up? What if I can't be good to her because I can't get Clare out of my mind?"

Hugh frowned, sitting up a bit straighter in his chair. "How I do it is by reminding myself that none of these arrangements are meant to last forever, and failing to carry on would mean the difference between having a full belly and eventually going hungry for lack of funds. Your situation will improve with time dedicated to your business, but until I can gain recognition for my art there is nothing else."

Of course, Hugh was right. It made perfect sense, which was how Edward knew he couldn't be thinking with his head just now. It was the damn organ in his chest, which had developed a tender spot for a bespectacled bluestocking with a penchant for collecting things and experimenting with flowers.

"I'm sorry," he said. "I don't know what I could be thinking. I've been a bit out of sorts."

"It sounds to me as if there's a very simple explanation for why you feel so out of sorts," Hugh said. "Her name is Clare."

Edward braced his elbows on the desk and his head in his hands with a groan. "Damn it. How did I allow this to happen? I've developed an infatuation for my keeper. Has anything like this ever happened to you?"

"I can't say I've ever felt anything other than affection for the women I've serviced. It is difficult to cater to someone in such a way without at least liking them. I never really felt as if I knew them, though, or that they knew me."

And therein lay the problem. He'd opened himself up to her that first night, and probed into the details of her life with his idiotic questions. Instead of keeping things light and easy, he'd gone and fallen headlong into a complication.

"It will pass," Hugh offered, though he didn't sound any more certain than Edward was. "She will eventually move on, and you'll be forced to do the same. As well, you should know Benedict is never happy to learn that one of us might be developing tender feelings for a client. It isn't good for business, and Benedict is nothing if not strictly business."

With a slow nod, Edward sat up straight and began pulling himself together. There was nothing for him to do but carry on and take things as they came. At this juncture, it was the best he could do—at least until the other aspects of his life found their way to some sort of normality.

"I understand," Edward replied. "It will not become a problem. I won't let it."

CHAPTER 8

That evening, Edward entered Clare's study, where he found her standing over an open box on one of her desks. As she paused to glance up at him with a smile, he realized the chest contained her collection of watches. She seemed to be in the middle of adding a new timepiece, one which she lifted from a smaller box before holding it up to the light for him to see.

"I purchased this beauty this afternoon," she said, her voice low and reverent. "Created in 1730 and made of solid gold, and look at this...there's a little *etui* here for snuff!"

She placed the heavy piece in his hands, and he held it up to the light, studying the delicate filigree scroll work adorning a chatelaine, which held the timepiece, several pearl charms, and the snuff container. He could imagine that amid the overblown wardrobe of a lady of 1730 such a piece would seem gaudy and excessive. But on its own it was quite exquisite.

"I've never seen anything like it," he replied, flipping open the watch to find its face adorned with a tiny painting of winged cherubs. "I can see why you'd want it for your collection."

His gaze wandered to the other watches resting on square compartments inside the chest. Brass, gold, and silver shined up at him as if they'd been recently polished, some boasting beaded or metal chate-laines, others adorned with glittering gemstones, and a few appearing quite plain on the surface. She seemed to collect indiscriminately, her collection comprised of both men's and women's timepieces.

"I wouldn't leave the antiquities shop until the proprietor gave it to me for a fair price. I was willing to pay what it was worth, but the man tried to rob me blind. In the end, he was convinced to see things my way."

Edward chuckled, imagining Clare staring down the antique dealer through her spectacles, her eyes gone cold as ice. She'd probably used her governess tone on him and made him feel three inches tall. The man had likely given her the watch at the price she wanted in an act of self-preservation.

"Congratulations on your triumph," he said, returning the watch to her and going back to study the others. "You've got quite a collection here."

She waved a hand toward the chest to indicate he was free to touch them. He lifted and examined a simple man's watch on a black silk ribbon. The watch itself, along with a seal, hung from a medallion comprised of a massive, clear diamond in a gold setting. Another—this one for a woman—hung from a gem-encrusted chatelaine, the stones arranged to look like the wings of butterflies. Some appeared to be decades or centuries old, and he was delighted to discover a sixteenth century clockwatch, a heavy thing comprised of brass to be worn on a chain about the neck.

"These are all so unique," he said, placing the old clockwatch back into its velvet housing with care. "They must have taken you ages to collect. Which one was your first?"

She took up the plainest watch in the bunch—a simple silver affair with a pattern of scrolls etched on the casing. Flipping it open, she revealed its cracked glass face and tiny sapphires resting where the numbers 12, 3, 6, and 9 would be.

"It isn't the most beautiful of the lot, or the oldest," she told him. "But it is my favorite because it belonged to my father."

She handed him the watch, which he handled with the utmost of care, not wanting to further damage something so important to her.

"Of course it's the most beautiful," he said. "That you love it so much makes it so."

She gave him a soft smile, then stared back down at the timepiece. "When my parents died, Alice and I were devastated. We spent those first days clinging to their things and weeping for hours. Alice was partial to one of Mother's handkerchiefs. It had been used to clean up spilled rose oil—mother's favorite scent. She'd hold it to her nose and inhale, then collapse into a fit of tears. I found Father's watch abandoned on the washstand and forgotten when he'd taken ill. He'd knocked it over in a delirious fit of fever, which is how the glass cracked. For months I carried this with me everywhere I went. I even slept with it beneath my pillow. Aunt Helene noticed and offered to have it fixed, but I wouldn't allow it. I wanted to keep it just the way he'd left it."

That would explain why this watch was the only imperfect one in the box, the others immaculately cared for.

"I have a collection of my father's waistcoats in a trunk at home," Edward told her, putting the watch back in its place. "I'll never be able to wear them unless I grow a bit rounder in the middle, but ... of all his things I latched onto those for some reason. His other things were sold because we needed the money, but Caroline kept one of his snuffboxes, and Jacob selected two of his tiepins. For me, it was too damned hard to part with those waistcoats."

With a sigh, she edged closer to Edward, reaching out to place a hand on his chest. "I'm sorry. You did not come here for me to draw you into trading morose stories about our fathers. And with your loss being so recent—"

"It's all right," he assured her, wrapping an arm around her waist and pulling her against him. "I'd rather talk about him than let his memory die. And you should feel free to talk to me about anything you wish."

"Still, I'd rather not ruin our evening with grief."

He brushed his lips against hers, one hand sliding down toward the curve of her arse. "Then we'll spend it doing something else."

"Yes," she replied, wrapping her arms around his neck and deepening the kiss.

All thought fled his mind and he succumbed to the same intoxicating effect he experienced whenever in Clare's presence. Nothing else mattered just then; not the inevitability of parting ways, or where he might go from there, or how it would feel to be banished from her life for good. The only thing that mattered just then was the taste of her, the feel of her body against his, and making sure she enjoyed herself as much as she had every other night before now.

He guided her closer to the hearth, where the clutter of their surroundings gave way to the patch of rug enclosed by her furniture. Their lips met again, and he drank from her mouth with a desperate longing, plunging his tongue in to entangle with hers. She clung to him, returning the kiss with an equal fervor.

They began tearing at one another's clothes, hands moving with swift, clumsy motions. She grunted in frustration against his lips while fumbling with his cravat, so he reached up to help her yank it loose. Tossing the linen aside, she attacked the buttons of his waistcoat while he worked the fastenings down the back of her gown. Garments flew in every direction until they sank to the floor together, completely bared.

Facing one another on their knees they pressed close, mouths meeting and parting, hands roaming. Her fingernails lightly scored his back, then she cupped his buttocks, urging him tighter against her. He dipped his head to seek out a nipple, drawing it into his mouth and sucking with deep pulls until she cried out, back arching to offer more of herself to him. After a while, she braced her hands against his chest, pushing him onto his haunches, then flat on his back. She crawled over him, thighs straddling his and hands braced on either side of his head. She wasn't wearing her spectacles, so he had a clear view of her eyes, dark blue and clear like the sky just after sunset.

She planted a swift kiss on his lips, then began trailing her way down his body, leaving shivers of delight in her wake. He threaded his fingers in her hair as her tongue circled hotly over his chest, teasing a nipple before she continued her slow path downward. His cock throbbed with anticipation, his entire body going tense as he waited for the first hot stroke of her tongue where he wanted it most.

He gasped when she took him into her mouth without hesitation, dragging her lips down then up his shaft in one fluid motion. Not the first time in the past fortnight she'd fucked him with her mouth, but Edward never ceased to be amazed at how readily she threw herself into passion, always giving as good as she got. He groaned, surging into her mouth with slow thrusts, heat and wetness enveloping him over and over in an excruciatingly slow drag.

"Christ, CeCe," he groaned, his eyes sliding closed as he gave himself over to ecstasy.

She moaned around him, pausing at his tip to swirl her tongue around his head before taking him in as far as he would go, drawing another hoarse cry from deep within him. He released her hair and reached down to toy with her breasts, gently tugging her nipples as she increased her rhythm, her head bobbing and her lips stroking him. Her breath quickened, low whimpers emitting from her as he pleasured her the only way he could with so much of her body out of his reach.

Taking hold of her face, he drew her off his cock, unable to help a chuckle at the way she glared at him as he fell free of her mouth.

"I wasn't finished yet," she grumbled.

Stroking her cheek, he smiled. "I don't want you to stop, love. I simply envy you for having all the fun. Turn around for me."

Her eyes went wide, then her expression turned sultry as she understood his meaning. He helped her arrange herself so she lay atop him, legs straddling his head and putting him in the perfect position. From the nest of dark curls cloaking her mons, the teasing glimpse of pink flesh made his mouth water and his arousal swell to painful limits. She moaned when he drew his tongue over her in one long lap, pressing against her clitoris, then making his slow way to her channel. He plunged his tongue inside her, his palate bathed with her earthy taste and his senses overwhelmed by the heady scent of her arousal.

Taking hold of his cock, Clare picked up where she'd left off, sucking him with rhythmic pulls that made his toes curl. He grasped her buttocks and spread her, revealing more of her cunny and taking aim at the swollen pink bud. His cock muffled her cry as he latched onto it and treated her to the same torment she exacted on him. Her wetness slicked his lips, and her hips began to undulate as she rode his tongue, seeking her own pleasure while giving him his. They moved together, him thrusting into her mouth and Clare rocking against him with wild abandon.

Never letting up with his mouth, he delved two fingers into her sheath and began to thrust at the same rhythm with which she sucked his cock. She released him from her mouth with a startled cry, her back arching to take him deeper. He slid in to his third knuckles, his fingers drenched in her juices as he fucked her with them the way he soon would with his cock.

A moment later, the wet rasp of her tongue against his bollocks nearly unmanned him. Sucking in a deep breath, he willed away climax and concentrated on taking her to the finish. She was close, shuddering atop him and her ministrations growing less adept. He quickened his fingers inside her, his lips pulling on her clitoris until she finally splintered. Throwing her head back, she groaned and shook, her cunt pulsating around his fingers as he stroked her through the climax. It seemed to go on and on, her thighs shaking and her voice growing hoarse as she came off like a flame stoked to a roaring inferno.

When at last she'd gone still with her head rested on his thigh and her breaths coming out in heavy pants, Edward turned her onto her back, then swiveled to come to rest between her legs. She seemed a world away, her eyes glassy as she recovered from her powerful climax. But, he couldn't wait another moment to be inside her, and her legs fell wide open as he lunged between them, aiming his cock at her slick opening. He fell into her with a growl, clenching his teeth and holding back from spilling inside her then and there.

He wanted to savor every moment of this and make it last, but she'd brought him close to spending with her mouth and he hovered close to the edge. Gathering her legs over his shoulders, he slid deeper and began rolling his hips, trying to go farther with every thrust. His body seemed as desperate as his mind to be so connected to her that they no longer felt like separate people and became like one being. She stoked to life again, fingers digging into the rug as his pace became faster, his body breaking out with a light sheen of sweat. He watched the way the firelight played over her bared skin, the bounce of her breasts with every stroke, the delirious expression of pleasure that transformed her face into one of the most glorious things he'd ever seen.

"CeCe, I—"

He clenched his teeth around the words that had nearly escaped him in a fit of madness.

I adore you.

I love you.

You've bewitched me beyond all reason.

Even as far gone as he was at the moment, he couldn't allow himself to tread that far and ruin what remained of their time together. She had given no indication of any such feelings for him, and might be repulsed to know he'd made more of their agreement than he ought. He needed to tread with more care until he unraveled all the desires and hopes she held inside.

"You feel so bloody good," he rasped instead, which was as much the truth as the other things he wanted to say.

"Yes, Edward," she mewled, raising her hips to meet his battering thrusts. "Yes!"

She splintered again, her back arching up off the rug as she released in a torrent of pulsating flesh, wetness, heat, and throaty moans of ecstasy. Edward followed soon after, pulling free of her just before his seed spilled from him, streaking his hand and her open thighs. Bracing himself over her, he hung his head and struggled to catch his breath. At the same time, he worked to get a hold of himself and chase these delusions of love from his mind. He told himself he was mad, and that even if his feelings were real she couldn't possibly feel the same way.

Opening his eyes, he groped about for his coat and withdrew his handkerchief from the breast pocket. He used it to clean her, then tossed it aside.

She opened her arms and he went to her, gathering her against him and turning so they lay facing each other, one of her legs draped over his. For a moment, he could have sworn he recognized something in her eyes—an answering sentiment to his own turbulent emotions. As if she might actually feel something as deep and real for him as he did for her. But then, she closed her eyes and burrowed her face in his chest, and he told himself he'd been mistaken. A trick of the light or wishful thinking, perhaps. He had obviously read what he'd seen all wrong.

Still, the longer he lay there holding her and realizing they'd come one day closer to parting ways, Edward found it difficult not to give in to the hope that perhaps he'd been right.

CHAPTER 9

Four more days passed Edward by without him finding the courage to ask Clare the question he'd been turning over in his mind ever since his meeting with Hugh and Benedict. It grew more imperative with each passing day to know whether she intended to extend their arrangement. He'd managed to gain back an important client for Norton & Rivers, with a shipment due to leave the London port in a few short weeks. Word had begun to spread that the line was back in business with a new owner at the helm, and while there was still much to be done, Edward foresaw a stunning comeback. All he needed was time and the funds to continue making improvements. And there would be no more money without Clare or another keeper filling his pockets.

But, the more he thought on the dilemma, the more he realized he simply could not do it. If he asked her for a few more months, then he'd want a year. If he got that year, he'd want more years. He'd want her life to become a part of his, her hand in marriage, the children she would bear him. But how could he ask those things of her when he could hardly afford to care for his siblings let alone a wife? How could he bear to discover that she might never come to love him as much as he loved her?

In the days following their desperate fucking on the floor of her study, he'd tried to convince himself that he was making too much of his feelings. He told himself it was an infatuation that would fade, that it had happened too quickly for him to be certain how he truly felt. But time to think had only affirmed what he knew to be sure. He wasn't certain when it had happened: when he first heard her laugh, their first kiss, the time he'd seduced her with scientific terms, or even the moment she'd laid her father's watch in his hands and told him why she clung to the broken timepiece. It didn't matter when or how, not when he could look back on each of those encounters with such emotion welling within his chest and tearing him apart.

He loved her, and no amount of denial would change that.

Which was why the best thing he could do was allow their association to end. He'd only torture himself being with her when he knew there could never be anything more. It would hurt, but time and distance could mend that. Eventually, he would be able to look back on their month together with wistful fondness.

He came to this final decision one afternoon while toiling away in his office, the dark gloom of a foggy day a match for his mood. All there was left to do was ask Benedict to find him a new keeper, preferably one who would want him for longer than a month.

He'd just set his quill aside and decided to take a walk to clear his head, when the door swung open. A woman stood silhouetted in the opening, and he recognized Clare before she'd even stepped into the light of the tapers. He'd know her anywhere—her form, her posture, the way she walked as she approached his desk.

Her bright smile only drove the dagger deeper into his heart, such a sharp juxtaposition to his own dark mood. She must have noticed the tightness of his mouth and the furrows in his brow, because she faltered, her smile fading a bit.

"Are you very busy?" she asked. "I suppose this could wait, but I have news and I couldn't wait to share it."

Schooling his face into a more neutral expression, he stood and rounded the desk toward her. He took her hand and kissed the back of it, lingering for a moment to draw in that soothing lavender and rosemary scent.

"I am never too busy for you," he said. "And your news must have been good for you to brave this ghastly weather to come visit me."

While she seemed to have heard him, her gaze had begun to wander, taking in the place that represented the livelihood of his family.

"So, this is where you spend your days," she murmured. "You've been working so hard. I hope things have begun to turn around for Norton & Rivers."

Leaning against the desk, he crossed his arms over his chest. "So far so good. Three of our ships are now in tiptop shape and ready for cargo. I managed to gain back a lost client and have met with a few prospective ones. Repairs on the rest of the vessels is getting on well and I have three full crews ready to sail."

That ready smile lit up her face once more and she clasped her hands against her chest. "I am happy for you. And I want to help you continue to make progress. That is why I've come. My news...you see, I've just left from meeting with Mr. Sterling on the matter of our contract."

Edward stiffened, his breath catching and holding as her words began to sink in. He felt torn in opposite directions, part of him hoping to hear the news he'd craved a week ago, the other part recoiling because he'd already decided this should not happen.

"I see," he managed, uncertain of what else to say.

She nodded, coming closer until they were nearly touching. He kept his arms crossed, needing some sort of barrier against her, or else he'd take her in his arms, kiss her senseless and beg her to love him.

"Yes," she replied. "I went to Mr. Sterling myself and asked him to draw up a new contract...one which doesn't have to end unless we want it to. That way, we can continue as we have been, and you needn't worry about where your income will come from while you work to get the line restored to its former glory."

He clenched his jaw, his stomach churning and quivering as he realized what she was saying. She wanted him, for far longer than a few months if he understood her correctly. But, she hadn't done this because she wanted *him*. She'd done it out of some sense of charity to keep him from living hand to mouth again. It left a bitter taste in his mouth, and an itchy tightness that seized him from head to toe. There was nothing deeper to it, for surely a woman who was falling in love would require an end to this unorthodox arrangement and be open to courtship?

"That was thoughtful of you," he murmured shaking with the will it took to stay composed. "But I can assure you that I need no such largess. You see, I've already decided to ask Benedict to find a new keeper for me."

Her mouth fell open and one hand came to her belly as if he'd struck her there. The urge to beg her forgiveness came over him hard and fast, but he pushed it away, determined to get out of this with his dignity intact. She had already made him love her and want her in a way he'd never wanted anyone or anything else. Now, he would stand here and endure the truth without letting on how much it hurt.

"Y-you want someone else?" she stammered, confusion and hurt melting away her previously joyous expression. "But I thought—"

"That I'd want to have a keeper who only endures my presence in her bed out of a sense of pity? I might be a courtesan, but I do have some dignity. If I'm going to service anyone, it'll be someone who actually wants *me*. So, thank you for your generous offer but I'm afraid I'll have to decline."

Her shock gave way to anger, her face flushing and her eyes flashing like strikes of lightning. "Is that what you think? That I've only decided to do this because I feel sorry for you?"

He shrugged, tearing his gaze away from her and staring across the room. "It's what you just said, isn't it? I suppose I cannot blame you. After all, my story is quite the pitiful one and I assume it made you feel responsible for me in a way. But, as I said, your pity is neither wanted nor needed."

Hands balled up at her sides, she glared at him, nostrils flaring. "You bloody idiot. You really have no idea, do you? God, you men are so daft! You wouldn't know the truth if it were spelled out for you using language a child could understand!"

Stunned, he dropped his arms and studied her closely. Her eyes had begun to glisten and she shook with anger. He realized his error too late, and a hard knot of regret had lodged itself in his throat.

"Clare," he whispered. "I thought...you never told me..."

"I didn't think I had to," she spat. "I would have thought it was as clear to you as it is to me, but I can see you are as dense as the rocks sitting in my study. I *love* you, you fool! And I thought that perhaps you might eventually come to love me. But we needed more time, and I thought...I hoped that if we had that time things would become clearer, and someday we might become more than courtesan and keeper."

The knot in this throat dropped down into his stomach, making him sick with the epiphany that he'd been entirely wrong. She was right; he was dense. He had seen the truth for himself, that night before the fire. But he'd convinced himself he'd been mistaken, and now that assumption would cost him dearly.

He reached out to take hold of her arm, trying to pull her into his embrace. "CeCe, wait. I'm sorry, I was mistaken—"

She jerked away from him with a sharp intake of breath, backing away from him as if she'd been burned. "And just what is so wrong with me wanting to help you with my money? My parents left it to me to do as I want, and it would have pleased me to help you. Are you so prideful that you would shun what I could offer you because you are a man and I am a woman? I thought you better than that, Edward, but clearly I am the one who is mistaken. It would be of no consequence if you were to marry me and take my inheritance as a dowry, would it? But, I offer to give you a piece of it because I love you—though God knows you don't deserve it—and you throw my offering back in my face!"

Edward made one last desperate attempt to touch her, to hold her and tell her he loved her until she grew sick of hearing it. But, she'd already turned for the door, leaving him behind with long, sure strides. He wanted to tell her he would marry her and damn the money, damn the contract, damn all of it. But as she turned in the doorway to look back at him, he saw that she'd pulled herself together. She now looked as if she were made of stone, her face implacable and her shoulders squared.

"Thank you for all the things you taught me," she said, her voice low and strained. "I hope you'll have a care with your next keeper. It isn't good business for you to go about stealing hearts and then breaking them."

"Clare..."

She was gone before he could get another word out, the door slamming behind her and rattling the walls. Edward fell against his desk with a swift sigh, the air knocked from him. His head spun with all that had changed in what felt like the blink of an eye. He had gone from despairing that Clare could never love him, to realizing she *did* love him but now he'd ruined everything.

"God damn it," he muttered, running a hand over his face.

He'd ruined his chances with Clare. What might have been a certainty had he kept his mouth shut had now been put out of his reach.

CLARE STORMED PAST HER AUNT AS SHE ENTERED THE TOWNHOUSE, her clothing damp from the thick fog descending over London like a dreary gray blanket. She supposed it was fitting to her mood, which had plummeted with a swiftness that left her reeling. It was a far cry from the hope she had felt after leaving the secret offices of the Gentleman Courtesans hidden away in the back of a modiste's shop. She hadn't been certain whether her plan would have the desired result, but she'd been willing to take that chance.

It had not taken her long to realize that she'd held back from making a decision concerning Edward out of fear. She had opened herself to passion and gained so much more in the process. Intimacy, companionship, *love*. She'd found it difficult to believe that Edward felt nothing for her, and had clung to the hope that more time would only strengthen the bond that had formed between them in a few short weeks. It had all seemed so simple to her. They needed more time for their connection to grow stronger, and Edward needed money. A longer arrangement had seemed like the perfect solution.

"CeCe, dear," Helene called out from the open drawing room door. "How did your meeting with Mr. Sterling go?"

Untying the ribbons of her sodden hat, she tossed it onto the entrance hall table beside the fresh flowers she'd arranged just this morning.

"Quite well, actually," she snapped, unable to keep the anger and hurt out of her voice. "It's been decided that Edward and I will not continue our arrangement. He will seek a new keeper and I will get on quite well without him."

She caught sight of her aunt's shocked expression just before spinning away to make for her greenhouse. The last thing she wanted was to have to explain her painful, embarrassing conversation with Edward.

"Wait, Clare! Won't you tell me what happened?"

"Suffice it to say, men are idiots," she threw over her shoulder without a look back.

She hated to treat her aunt so poorly, but if she spoke of it she might fall apart. She might fall to the floor, lay her head in Helene's lap and weep over what she'd come to want most but would never have. It was bad enough that Edward had seen her shed tears; she was done weeping for him. For God's sake, she was an educated woman, a wordly woman, a botanist! She had never been the sort to lapse into tears over a man and she would not start now.

Throwing open the door to the conservatory, she breathed a small sigh of relief. At least here, the only thing that mattered was the life she'd cultivated from soil and seeds. Her experiments might be unpredictable at times, but they did not have the power to ruin her life or hurt her. Trying again wouldn't expose her to more hurt or mortification.

Sinking down onto her stool, she noticed that one of her hybrids had begun to bud. Blossoms would be soon to follow, allowing her to see the results of her experiment. This should have brought her some sort of happiness, but she couldn't feel anything just now. She felt as if she'd been gutted, turned inside out with all her nerves exposed to the elements. What had once seemed so trivial to her—marriage, a family of her own, and the sort of love she'd never believed in—had become a most ardent wish, one that had been trampled on before it ever saw the light of day.

Taking a deep breath, she closed her eyes and allowed herself to feel it all for a moment. She would let herself be disappointed, angry, and heartbroken, but only until she was ready to leave this room. She had lived a life of contentment and independence before him, and she would do it again. Going forward, she would simply think of this as one of her experiments. Except, this particular test would never be repeated. It simply wasn't worth the result.

The sound of footsteps approaching had her opening her eyes and sitting up straight, to better conceal how wretched she felt. It was one thing to wallow in her misery alone, but quite another to let someone else bear witness to it—even Aunt Helene, who stood on the other side of the table peering at Clare with concern in her eyes.

"This morning you left here in a downright giddy mood, telling me you were off to extend your contract with Edward," she said. "Something happened between now and then."

Reaching for her journal, Clare flipped it open and recorded the date for a new entry. Avoiding her aunt's gaze, she began notating the growth and progress of her budding *Lilium*.

"Something did happen, but it wasn't of any consequence. I simply realized that you were right...some people are only meant to be a temporary part of our lives. That is all," she murmured, hating that her voice betrayed her on the last few words by cracking.

Seeming to sense that Clare would say no more on the matter, Helene sighed and retreated, leaving her in blessed solitude once more. As she went back to her notes, she repeated those words to herself over and over again, determined that she'd think and speak them as many times as it took for her to believe them.

CHAPTER 10

A few days later, Clare sat at her desk with a new letter from Gillian, this one having just arrived from Sussex. With it had come only one small mineral sample, but it might just be the most beautiful Clare had ever seen. 'Hastings firestorm amber' Gilly had called it, and the bit of it she'd sent seemed alive with tongues of flame from the inside. Holding the specimen up to the light, she observed the threads of red, orange, and brown effusing through the honey-colored stone, the light reflecting off its inner prisms like sparks.

Her friend's letter had been filled with news and cheer, which Clare had been glad to read no matter how it reminded her of her own recent disappointment. The Young siblings had departed Cornwall for Sussex, taking up at a seaside resort in Hastings for a bit of a holiday before moving on to their next destination. But Gilly was never capable of true rest for long, and she'd begun digging about the shingled shore in search of various treasures. It was here she had dug up the amber, a bit of which she'd sent to Clare. The two were enjoying the sea air as well as a respite from the constant pace of their work. As well, Randall had met a lovely young woman and the two seemed to be in the midst of a budding romance. That last bit of news would have relieved Clare a month ago, a sure sign that Gilly's brother had finally turned his attentions elsewhere. Yet, knowing that there were two people in Sussex falling in love while she was in London nursing a broken heart only annoyed her.

Because, of course it was so easy for other people. People who fit into each other's lives with ease, people who weren't eccentric blue-stockings or impoverished courtesans with failing shipping companies, and who knew how to give, receive and express love without tearing each other to pieces.

Edward isn't torn to pieces, she told herself with a derisive snort. *He's too busy saddling his high horse.*

His assumption that she'd only wanted to extend their arrangement out of pity angered her most of all. She had thought he'd come to know her better than that, but she'd obviously been mistaken. He didn't know her at all if her actions had sent him leaping to such an asinine conclusion. It was for the best, then. If he did not know her, he could not possibly love her.

Folding Gilly's letter and setting it aside, she then rose to retrieve the chest containing her minerals to store the amber. Just as she opened the latch and lifted the lid, the sound of voices came at her from downstairs. Inclining her head, she listened more closely, certain she recognized the male voice that seemed to penetrate the doors, vibrate the walls, and send unwanted pangs of longing straight to her traitorous heart.

She crept on silent feet to the stairs, peering over the railing at the landing below. Sure enough, she found Edward standing just within the entrance hall with his hat in his hands, his expression earnest as he spoke with Aunt Helene.

"Do you think she will see me?" he asked. "I don't know if she's informed you of what happened when last we spoke—"

"No," Helene said. "But whatever you said or did to her, she hasn't been herself these past few days. I am not certain allowing you to see her would be a good idea."

Clare bit her lip, wondering just what Edward could want with her now. He'd made it clear that he intended to move on with a new keeper. It seemed all had been said and done, yet here he stood, all but begging Helene to be allowed to see her.

"I just want the chance to make things right. She's capable of deciding for herself whether she wants to see me."

Helene looked ready to protest again, but curiosity got the best of Clare and she made her presence known by clearing her throat, the sound echoing down to the entrance hall. Two heads tilted upward, and her aunt grimaced at the sight of her, while Edward took on a look of sheer determination.

"CeCe," he said, his voice heavy and thick as if he were as over-wrought as she felt.

He looked ghastly, with dark circles showing beneath his eyes and his mouth pinched. From where she stood, he looked as if he hadn't slept in days. Could that be due to guilt, perhaps?

"Edward," she replied, fighting to keep her voice neutral. "You wished to speak to me?"

He nodded, taking a few steps toward the stairs before halting as if uncertain. "If you'll hear me out. It will only take a moment, I promise. When I'm finished, you are welcome to throw me out. Just...please listen to what I have to say."

She traded glances with Helene, who gave an exaggerated shrug as if to say, 'the devil if I know what you should do.'

Clare knew she had no choice but to speak with him. Words had flown between them so fast and without much thought the last time they spoke, and there were so many things to hash out. Most of all, she couldn't stand to let him leave without finding out why he'd come. The wondering would drive her mad before long.

"Very well," she said, gesturing for him to come upstairs.

His shoulders sagged as if in relief, and he climbed the steps, then preceded her into the study. Closing the door, Clare leaned against it and watched as Edward paced away from her, then back to the center of the room.

Running his fingers through his mussed hair, he heaved a sigh and plunged ahead. "Hypothesis: if a man loves a woman but is uncertain she feels the same, said man convinces himself he stands no chance for a real future with her. Conclusion: the man is an oblivious dolt."

Her stomach began tying itself in knots, her mind latching onto the first words he'd said. It was a wonder she'd heard the rest of it, because that first declaration echoed and resounded through her with overwhelming force.

If a man loves a woman...

"I'm sorry for what I said when I thought things were different. Even if I believed that, I should never have been so callous. It's just that...the thought of being with you, seeing you every day and loving you so much it hurts would kill me by degrees. I couldn't agree to more months, more years, without wanting more from you, Clare. And I do want more. I want everything, even knowing I have absolutely nothing to offer you."

Wringing her shaking hands, she stepped away from the door, coming closer and peering deep into his jade eyes. "I had told myself the same thing—that you couldn't possibly feel what I felt after so short a time. But, then I decided more time could change things, that eventually the 'more' I wanted would become possible. I was willing to take that chance, and I didn't care about the money or your circumstances. It's all just peripheral nonsense, Edward. The only thing that mattered to me was you."

Cupping her face with both hands, he leaned down until his forehead rested against hers, his gaze burning into hers with an intensity that left her breathless.

"I love you. It shouldn't surprise me that it's happened so swiftly, because that's what you've done since the moment I met you, CeCe. You took me by surprise and you've continued to do so every day I've known you. I know I am not a good match for you. I'm the impoverished owner of a shipping company with an uncertain future. I have very little money that hasn't been sunk into Norton & Rivers. I met you as a desperate courtesan whose last resort was to warm the bed of a woman I didn't know just to be able to feed my family. I—"

"You are selling yourself short," she interrupted, reaching up to put a finger over his lips. "All those things might be true, but you've forgotten a few other important details. Such as your willingness to accept me as I am when so many other people have shunned me as an oddity. And there is your strength under duress, where many other men would have watched their lives fall down around them in despair. But, you discovered a way to make things right for your family, and no lengths were too great. Then, there is the most important thing of all: that your efforts brought you to me."

He smiled, then pressed a kiss against her fingertips. "That, I will never regret."

"Do you know what a geode is, Edward?"

"No, but I'd love for you to explain it. You know how I feel about all those scientific terms."

She huffed a laugh, but then grew serious once more. "A geode is a rock that looks rather plain and unremarkable on the outside, but when sawed open, it is revealed to contain minerals inside—amethyst, quartz, jasper, celesite, the most beautiful crystals you've ever seen. That is what I think of when I consider how all this has happened. I viewed intimacy as being akin to that plain rock—nothing special, something I could live without. But you opened up an entire world of possibilities to me, and now I can see deeper. I can see everything I would have missed had I passed you over like some common bit of stone. There is nothing common about you, and you have more important things to offer than material comforts. I have possessed those things my entire life, so I have no need of them from you. But there are other things I need, and I only want them with you."

He took her into his arms, and she sank into his embrace, all her previous hurt and fear melting away. She realized now that the proposed second contract should never have happened. Had she been brave enough, she would have simply told him the truth of her heart and trusted that it would lead her to where they were now. But, they'd both made their mistakes, and now was the time for making things right.

"Say it again," he whispered between kisses, his teeth playfully nipping at her lower lip. "The first time you said it, you were angry and hurt. I want to hear it again without all that tainting it."

Threading her fingers through his hair, she placed a swift kiss on his lips, the tip of his nose, then right between his eyes. "I love you, Edward. I love you madly, deeply, and truly."

He captured her lips again, tightening his hold on her and lifting her off her feet. She clung to him wrapping her arms around his neck and her legs around his waist, groaning as his nearness stoked a desperate desire in her. It had only been days since she'd seen him last, but she was starved for him—for his touch, his kiss, his voice whispering words of love and scientific expressions into her ear.

"I've a hypothesis for you now," she said as he sank into the nearest chair with her, arranging her comfortably on his lap.

She curled up against him, fitting her head beneath his chin and nuzzling his neck. He stroked a hand down her back and kissed the top of her head.

"What's that, love?"

"If two people who love each other and never want to be parted, they will be married as soon as possible."

Tipping her chin up so she looked him in the eye, Edward gave her that heartwarming, boyish smile she'd come to love more than any sight in the world.

"Conclusion: the man and the woman will live happily together until death do them part."

EDWARD WINCED AS HE TOOK IN BENEDICT'S REDDENED FACE AND thunderous countenance. Hugh had offered to sit in on the final meeting between the two men while they hashed out the reasons for Edward parting ways with the Gentleman Courtesans. As he had assumed, Benedict was not thrilled by the news of his and Clare's upcoming nuptials.

"Let me ensure I understand you correctly," Benedict ground out, cool blue eyes narrowed murderously at him. "Miss Dunnaby was just here a week ago to sign a new contract, after which she wrote a bank draft for a substantial amount of money...and you are here to tell me that instead of being her courtesan you are now going to *marry her*?"

Shifting in his chair, Edward crossed one leg over the other. "Well, that's putting it a bit simply but, in short, yes."

Benedict fairly seethed, his knuckles turning white as he balled his hands up on the surface of his desk. "So now, not only am I short one courtesan as well as one of the most lucrative contracts this agency has ever seen, I must now ensure future clients understand that this is a courtesan agency and not a fucking matchmaking service."

Edward and Hugh both flinched as his voice rose on the last few words, fairly shaking the small secret office off the back of Madame Hershaw's dress shop.

"Ben, this does not have to be as bad as you are making out to be," Hugh reasoned. "Miss Dunnaby seems like a discreet sort, so I highly doubt she will go about telling everyone how she met her fiancé."

Benedict snorted and rolled his eyes. "Of course you'd think of it as being that simple. But the fact of the matter remains that your job as a courtesan is to bed your keeper and make her happy enough to keep us all flush in the pockets. If all of you start getting it in your heads that you're in love and want to marry your keepers, we'll be ruined within a year."

"I understand your position entirely," Edward replied. But none of this was done on purpose, and I certainly never thought that entering into this agreement would lead to me finding the woman I want to marry. I won't pretend to regret a bit of it, because I don't."

"Of course you don't," Benedict snapped, waving a dismissive hand in Edward's direction. "I gave you the chance to better your circumstances, but you decide to marry the chit to get your hands on her fortune instead."

Edward came to his feet, having reached the edge of his patience with Benedict. He would admit the man had a reason to be a bit miffed, but he'd just gone too far.

"Her fortune had nothing to do with it, so I'll thank you not to imply such again."

Benedict scoffed, rising to his feet and inclining his head at the door. "Get out of my sight. Inform your betrothed that her bank draft will be burned and she needn't worry I'll deposit the funds. If you whisper a word about my agency or mention the names of myself or Hugh, you'll regret it."

Taking hold of his arm, Hugh drew Edward toward the door. "Come, it's best to leave him alone when he's like this. He's angry now, but he will come to see reason soon enough."

Edward put the other man behind him, not giving a damn if Benedict ever stopped being infuriated with him. They'd never been more than acquaintances, and aside from being responsible for bringing Clare into his life the Gentleman Courtesans had only ever been meant to be a temporary part of his life.

Exiting the modiste's shop through a back door, he and Hugh stepped out into an alley, then followed it out into Cavendish Square. Hugh turned to him then, a wide smile on his face.

His mood had lifted now that he was out of Benedict's presence. How could he feel anything other than joy at knowing Clare would be his wife?

"I suppose congratulations are in order. Can I expect an invitation to your wedding?

"The banns will be read for the first time this coming Sunday," he replied. "And of course you can expect to be invited. You are partially responsible for me finding CeCe, after all. Though, I do hope this does not cause a rift between you and Benedict. You did vouch for me."

"He can't stay angry with me forever…I'm one of his best courtesans. Perhaps I'll avoid recommending any new men in the future."

"That might be best," Edward quipped. "Thank you, my friend. You helped me when I was at my lowest point, and I will always be grateful for that."

"Think nothing of it. I know how it feels to be desperate, so I was happy to help. I look forward to receiving that invitation."

With that, they parted ways, Hugh heading off in the direction of the Strand and Edward making his way home. Caroline was waiting for him to convey her to Clare's townhouse, where his sister and his fiancée would meet for the first time. His sister had been elated to learn that he was soon to be wed and couldn't wait to meet the woman who would become her sister-in-law. Apparently having two brothers had left her longing for a female sibling, yet another good thing to come out of this marriage. As he loped along searching for a hackney coach, Edward decided nothing but good things could come from a union with the woman he loved. For the first time in years, his future seemed brighter and more certain than ever.

CHAPTER 11

The wedding of Miss Clare Dunnaby to Mr. Edward Norton occurred on a warm day at the end of spring, an intimate ceremony held at St. Martin-in-the-Fields. Jacob stood with Edward as the best man, while Clare's friend Gillian had arrived from Sussex just in time to act as a maid-of-honor.

Clare had walked down the aisle on the arm of Helene, whom she had asked to give her away for lack of a living father. It might be a bit unorthodox, but Helene had been her sole parent for most of her life. It wouldn't have felt right to have anyone else walk her down the aisle to her waiting groom.

Edward's face had transformed into a mask of delighted shock and awe as she'd approached, wearing a gown of pure white net laid over powder blue silk and adorned with minimal flounces of blond lace along the hem. The white netting fell open at the front to trail behind her as she walked, white gloves covering her to the elbow. In her hands she held a bouquet made primarily of her hybrid *Lilium*, which had bloomed with the most pleasing effect. They had the hardy composition of the Madonna lily with the brilliant colors of the tiger lily—fading from bright orange at the center to brilliant white at the tips of the petals, with the tiger lily's signature black spots.

He'd been resplendent himself in black with white linen, a blue waistcoat matching her gown and offering relief from the stark colors. His eyes had shone with open admiration and love as she'd met him at the altar to join him in the recitation of their vows.

The ceremony had been followed by the wedding breakfast in what was now Edward and Clare's new Town residence. Clare had been reluctant to part ways with Helene, even if her new home was only a few minutes' carriage ride away. But, her aunt had insisted that she would get on just fine living alone, even joking that it would be easier for her to engage in her clandestine affairs without Clare underfoot.

"Besides, I shall have plenty of excuses to visit you whenever I wish. After all, I expect to become a great-aunt soon."

Helene had also revealed that apart from her inheritance, there was still a dowry that had been left by her father. At her shock upon learning this, her aunt had simply shrugged and informed her that she'd never given up hope that Clare would someday wed. The inheritance she'd gained had been a separate arrangement, to become hers at the age of twenty-one whether she was wed or not. Which meant they now had the perfect solution for the problem of Norton & Rivers. While Edward had confessed to not liking the idea of using her dowry to finish paying off his debts and inject more capital into the line, Clare had been firm that she wouldn't marry him unless he agreed to do just that. Thanks to her inheritance, she now had more money than she could ever spend in a lifetime, and he had no reason to feel guilty over all of it becoming his now that they were wed.

Caroline would take up residence with them, and Jacob had been convinced to abandon his bachelor's lodgings as well. Edward had recently taken his brother on as a protégé, teaching him the ins and outs of the business as he worked to rebuild it from scratch. The sign outside the dockyard office now read: Norton & Norton Line, with the anticipation that once Jacob knew what he was about, he would come in as a full-on business partner.

Gilly and Randall had returned after receiving their invitation to the wedding. They had convinced Clare and Edward to accompany them on their travels once a secretary was hired given the business was becoming stable enough to do without constant management. They were soon to be off to the fossil-rich coast of Devon, a place Clare had always wished to explore. It would be a wedding trip of sorts, one that struck Clare as being more perfect than one of the fashionable destinations. Walking the moors and staring over rocky cliffs with her new husband would be the most romantic experience of her life.

After a long day of eating and toasting over champagne, then seeing their guests out, Edward and Clare had spent the afternoon resting and recovering from their whirlwind of a wedding and enjoying the freedom of being together in their own home.

That evening, she left the washroom adjacent to their bedroom to find Edward waiting for her before the hearth with a small wooden box in his hands. Adoration overwhelmed her. She didn't think there would ever be a time she could look upon him without her stomach erupting into mad flutters or her blood heating with desire. The firelight made his hair gleam like bronze, his eyes appearing like dark emeralds in the dim lighting of the room.

"I have a wedding gift for you," he declared, extending the box to her. "It took me weeks to find just the right thing, but when I saw this I knew it was perfect."

Thinking of her own gift nestled in the pocket of her dressing gown, she smiled. "What a coincidence. I have something for you, too."

"Mine first," he insisted, his gaze lighting with excitement as he watched her open the box.

Nestled inside was one of the most stunning watches she'd ever seen. The outer casing was made of brilliant gold ringed with iridescent pearls, in the center of which sat a vivid enamel painting of an angel surrounded by billowy white clouds, her wings outstretched. She opened the watch to find a pristine white face, and more of the perfect pearls and delicate gold hands ticking away the minutes. From it hung a matching chatelaine.

"Oh, Edward...it's stunning."

"It isn't as old as some of your other watches. But I knew you would appreciate the workmanship as well as the artistry of it. Now you are one purchase closer to your fiftieth watch."

After taking a moment to study his beautiful gift, she set it back inside its box and laughed while reaching into her dressing gown pocket.

"Actually, I still have a few more watches to collect to reach fifty. You see, I've decided it was time to part ways with one of them."

She placed her gift in his hand and stood back to watch him study it. She hadn't bothered to wrap it or put it in a box, wanting to feel the transfer of the silver from her hand to his as she gave him her most precious possession.

Edward frowned, then his face eased into shock as he ran a finger over the shining silver casing. "Your father's watch? Clare, I cannot accept this."

Placing a hand over his atop the watch, she nodded. "You can and you will. It is too important to go on sitting in a box collecting dust, and no one is more important to me than you. See, I had it repaired, so the glass is no longer cracked and it tells time quite accurately."

She opened the watch, displaying the new circle of glass enclosing the face. Then, she closed the watch again and turned it over so he could see the inscription engraved onto the back of the casing.

Love Always, Clare

"Ah, CeCe," he whispered, closing his hand around the watch and pulling her against him with one arm. "It's the best gift anyone's ever given to me. I'll take good care of it, I promise."

"I know you will," she replied, pressing a kiss to his jaw. "I trust you with it just like I trust you with everything else—my heart and soul, my life."

"I'll treasure them all, my bride," he replied, nuzzling her hair and planting a kiss atop her head. "Forever and always."

"I find it very telling that we exchanged identical wedding gifts," she said as the thought occurred to her suddenly. "Surely that must mean something—a sure sign that we are fated to be together."

"Fate is all well and good," Edward replied, setting his new watch upon the mantle, then prizing the box from her hand and setting it beside the timepiece. "But at the moment I am more interested in science. Chiefly, whether or not you are exhibiting the signs of arousal. I believe an examination is in order."

With a wicked grin, she began backing away from him, her fingers coming to the sash of her dressing gown. "I suppose I will allow that... all in the name of science, of course."

His eyes grew heavy-lidded and his lips parted as she dropped the robe to the floor to reveal that she wore nothing underneath.

"This will require research," he rasped, stalking her as she backed toward the bed. "Vigorous research."

Climbing up onto the bed, she lay back and crooked her finger at him. "What are you waiting for?"

She collapsed into a fit of giggles as he rushed to bed and came atop her with a leap, the sounds of her joy echoing through the chamber.

EPILOGUE

EXETER, DEVON

1819, 1 YEAR LATER ...

"Sir, you have a visitor...a Mr. and Mrs. Radcliffe."

Edward glanced up from the letter from Caroline and frowned. He'd just received the missive and had sat in the library to read the news out of London. He and Clare had left his sister in the care of Helene, who'd acted as a chaperone during the recently ended Season. His sister had been filled with exciting details of various outings and balls, as well as a gentleman she'd met and come to grow quite fond of. He'd just gotten to the part where she'd begun to fill him in on how Jacob was managing the business in his absence.

Edward and Clare had purchased a country home in Exeter after traveling here with Gillian and Randall Young and falling in love with the landscape. The fresh, seaside air proved a much-needed reprieve from crowded, foggy London, while the rocky beaches and cliffs offered Clare the perfect opportunity to explore and excavate to her heart's content. Apparently, Devon proved a hotbed of fossils and minerals, which she and Gillian took great joy in unearthing and classifying together.

Things seemed to be going well enough in London without him, so Edward was content to linger in their new home for as long as Clare wanted to—especially given the new discovery of her delicate condition.

He stood and turned to find her standing in the doorway, one hand pressed to the small mound swelling at her middle. It was still early yet, but the signs of her pregnancy had begun to show a little over a month ago, and now she was growing, proclaiming for the world that she carried his child inside her.

"See them into the yellow salon," Clare instructed the butler, before allowing the servant to pass.

"Did I hear that correctly?" she asked once they were alone. "Hugh is here, and he brought someone with him?

Edward ran a hand over his jaw, still reeling from what he'd just heard. "He did say Mr. Radcliffe, and he also mentioned a Mrs., but the last I'd heard Hugh was still working as a courtesan. Unless he…no, it can't be. It must be his mother or one of his sisters. But then, his family cut him off years ago, so that isn't possible, either."

Taking his hand and beaming at him with her wide smile, she tugged him toward the door. "Well, there is only one way to find out for certain, isn't there?"

Edward followed her from the room. The butler had announced Mr. and Mrs. Radcliffe as if speaking of a husband and wife, but that defied everything Edward knew to be true.

However, as they entered the room to greet their visitors, Edward was stunned to find Hugh seated beside a lovely young woman who was neither his mother nor one of his sisters. With porcelain skin and sable hair, she peered at him with shy, dark eyes, her cheeks turning a pretty pink as Hugh came to his feet.

"Edward, I do hope we aren't imposing. We happened to be in Devon visiting Evie's mother, when I remembered your last letter. I wanted to see you and make an introduction."

Tearing his gaze away from the woman, Edward gaped at his friend in wide-eyed shock, fumbling for words.

"I...you...I don't understand."

"Forgive his rudeness," Clare spoke up, coming forward and offering a smile to Hugh and his companion. "It is good to see you again, and of course you are welcome here anytime." Turning her gaze to the silent woman, she inclined her head. "I'm Mrs. Clare Norton, and this is my husband, Edward."

Hugh returned her smile, then offered a hand to the seated woman and urged her to her feet. "I am glad to see you again, as well, Clare. May I introduce my wife, Mrs. Evelyn Radcliffe."

Edward's jaw dropped as his suspicion was proven true, and his wife began trading pleasantries with the other woman. He met Hugh's gaze, and his friend gave him a sheepish smile.

"Quite a surprise, I know, but it all happened too fast for me to update you by letter. I decided a visit and explanation in person would be best."

Shaking off his stunned stupor, he turned to Evelyn and offered his hand. "Mrs. Radcliffe, it is an honor to meet you. Hugh is a boor who has told me absolutely nothing about you."

Her blush deepened, but she offered a tentative smile and placed her hand in his. "Please, call me Evelyn. And I told Hugh he ought to write first, but he insisted he wished to surprise you."

"Well you've certainly done that," he remarked, turning back to Hugh. "I leave London for a few months and you go and get yourself leg-shackled?"

Hugh chuckled as Clare urged them to sit and went to send for refreshments. "You may now count me as the second courtesan to find himself married to his keeper. Perhaps Benedict was right to worry after all."

Edward sank into an armchair with a grimace. "God, he'll never stop blaming me."

"Perhaps not," Hugh agreed before turning an adoring glance on his wife. "But, like you, I cannot bring myself to regret it."

Clare joined them just as a flock of footmen entered carrying trays laden with a tea service and various refreshments. As she poured for everyone, Edward turned to Hugh.

"All right, out with it. I want to know everything."

Slouching on the loveseat, he braced an arm along the back of it behind his wife, who nestled closer to him. "Well, it is a long story..."

⁂

Hugh's 'long story' continues in Portrait of a Lady, out now. Click here to download!

THE GENTLEMAN COURTESANS
SERIES READING ORDER

Now Available:

Tempting the Bluestocking (prequel novella)

Portrait of a Lady

What a Courtesan Wants

Making of a Scandal

Taming of the Rake

Chasing Benedict

ABOUT THE AUTHOR

Sexy heroes ... sassy heroines ... electrifying erotic romance.
Victoria Vale has written over two dozen Romance and Young Adult novels under various pseudonyms. As a lover of erotic romance, she enjoys nothing more than a sexy hero paired with a sassy heroine, flavored with a dash of spice and lots of heat. A wife and mother of three, she enjoys reading (of course), cooking, sewing ... and other activities that aren't appropriate for inclusion in a biography.